NEWPORT NUPTIALS

CINDY NICHOLS

PRICKLY PEAR PRESS

Copyright © 2023 by Cindy Nichols

All rights reserved.

No part of this book may be reproduced in any form or by any electronic or mechanical means, including information storage and retrieval systems, without written permission from the author, except for the use of brief quotations in a book review.

CHAPTER 1

Sawdust swirled in the air, just like it had been for over a month at Jen Watson's house. She held her hand over her mouth as she swiped a wet rag over the chairs on the deck. It wasn't the first time she'd done it and it wouldn't be the last, but she was certain she'd done it more often in the last month than ever in her life at her grandmother's Newport Beach house that was now hers. Well, not exactly hers, but close enough for now.

She hadn't expected that when she'd come to the house in June to stay for the summer that she'd never leave. And that her long-time friend Faith would start a pillow business and be staying at the house with her.

She shook her head, marveling at how things had all turned out. Just as she finished wiping off the chairs and trying to fluff the dust out of her hair, she thought she heard a voice over the balcony.

"Hi, Mrs. Grover," she said, waving at her elderly neighbor. She raised her eyebrows at Mrs. Grover's newly coiffed hair, white clamdiggers and cute, powder blue sweater. And was that lipstick she had on? That had to be a first.

"Hello, Jen," Mrs. Grover said, smiling up at Jen and glancing over at the downstairs window into the kitchen. She rose onto her tiptoes, glancing in the other window.

It took a minute, but Jen finally understood why Mrs. Grover was all dressed up—and why she was on Jen's sidewalk at all. "Oh, Earl and Keith knocked off a little early today. They had to go get more supplies. But they sure made a mess while they were here."

Jen swung the dust cloth against the railing of the balcony, sending a plume of dust in Mrs. Grover's direction, and Mrs. Grover took a quick sidestep to avoid it.

"Oh, sorry about that." Jen set the rag in the corner and turned back toward Mrs. Grover. "Meet me in what's left of the kitchen. I'll head down."

A minute later, Jen and Mrs. Grover were in the kitchen, and Mrs. Grover said right away, "Whatever makes you think I was looking for Earl? Or I mean Earl and Keith? I just wanted to say hello."

Jen bit her tongue before she could say what she was thinking—that maybe it was the lipstick, or the fact that Mrs. Grover brought Earl and his son, Keith, cookies regularly and cooked for them the most evenings. But she didn't want to embarrass Mrs. Grover, who so far had vociferously denied that they were anything more than friends.

"It looked like you wanted to say something. What was it?"

"Oh, well, nothing, I guess." Mrs. Grover smiled, opting not to divulge anything—if there was anything to divulge. Mrs. Grover looked around and made a tsk-ing sound. Jen looked up at her neighbor, not sure what she was tsk-ing about.

Mrs. Grover surveyed the kitchen—the empty spaces where cabinets should be, the floor in the living room that was half-tile, half scraped concrete.

Jen handed Mrs. Grover a platter of appetizers that she'd made, since it was Friday and her best friends Carrie and Faith would be over for happy hour any minute, as they'd agreed that this evening would be when they'd plan the baby shower that her son, Michael, had asked Jen to plan for his wife. Well, Faith did live there, but she'd spent the day with Gary—or was it Gene? She'd been dating Gary and friends with Gene. At least, that's what Jen surmised. She wasn't sure, but knew Faith would fill her in later, and she should be home any minute.

Carrie breezed in, wine in hand. She looked around quickly and then over to Jen. "Wow, since they got that tile saw, they've really been at it, haven't they?"

Jen had had to wait for ages to get the flood damage repaired and had been without a kitchen for over a month now. And her good humor about it had just about run out, if it hadn't already.

"Yes, they have. They've been working really hard, and they promised that they'll be done in time for the shower."

She turned to Mrs. Grover and said, "You were going to say something, Mrs. Grover?"

Mrs. Grover's tugged at her earring. "Who, me? No, I wasn't. Yes, it looks like they've been working hard."

"Oh. I thought you were tsk-ing, which is usually followed by some sort of statement." Jen glanced at Carrie and held in her laugh, but Carrie didn't. "Mrs. Grover, you really should never, ever play poker. Really."

Mrs. Grover looked surprised and objected. "I'm a master bridge player. That takes some facial mastery."

"Hm. Facial mastery. That's an interesting way to put it," Carrie said, taking the chilled wine bottle and glasses from Jen and turning to follow her upstairs.

"Come on, Mrs. Grover, join us for happy hour. We have to talk about the baby shower we're supposed to plan for Michael. His mother-in-law was supposed to do it but she's apparently abandoned ship."

Mrs. Grover carried the platter up the stairs behind Jen. "So you're the cavalry?" she asked.

"Apparently," Jen replied. "But we've done it before." Carrie laughed and rolled her eyes.

That's an understatement. We had to pull off an entire wedding at the very last minute. They were lucky they had food for the guests. And I ended up acting as the bartender, if you can believe that."

Mrs. Grover's eyes widened as Jen and Carrie explained all the other things that had gone wrong with Michael and Amber's wedding that they'd had to cover for.

"The weird thing is that all along, Amber's mom said it

was handled. Flowers, photographer, all of it. And it wasn't."

"Oh, my," Mrs. Grover said. "And how did she respond when no flowers arrived and you had to do it?"

"Boy, did we have to scramble," Carrie said, shaking her head slowly.

"And as I recall, all she did was shrug her shoulders. Like oops, with a big smile on her face."

"I can't even imagine," Mrs. Grover said, taking the glass of wine that Carrie offered her. "I'd have blown my top."

Jen laughed. "We didn't have time for that. But I will say that there were a few choice words about Greta Blake afterward. Lucky she wasn't anywhere nearby."

"How'd she get put in charge of something like this again?" Mrs. Grover asked.

"I think Amber asked her. It's pretty common for the mom to do the shower, isn't it?"

Carrie shrugged. "Maybe in a normal world, but this is not a normal world, with her involved. This is going to be much easier. And will save us from having to scramble at the end again. It's just better if we have it here."

"Have what where?" Faith asked as she came out on the deck and held her empty wine glass in Carrie's direction.

"The baby shower," Carrie said as she filled Faith's glass. Jen sighed when Faith's eyebrows rose and she laughed.

"Here? Here, here? Where there are no floors, no cabinets, no appliances?" She patted her chair cushion a few times before she sat down on it, plumes of dust billowing out. "And sawdust in every nook and cranny?"

Jen squared her shoulders and knocked a bit more dust out of her hair. "I asked Earl and Keith if they thought they could get it done and they said yes. So I'm going with that."

Mrs. Grover looked over the balcony where stacks of lumber sat next to the rose garden and Jen's new stove. That was still in the box. Next to the new refrigerator that was also in a box. "Well, hope springs eternal," she said, lifting her wine glass along with her eyebrows.

CHAPTER 2

An hour later, they had a list of things that needed to be done, from invitations and favors to games and food. They also had a list of things they needed to talk to Amber and Michael about—like the gift registry. The only thing they had left to do was to divvy it up. Jen was feeling a bit better about the whole thing when her phone rang.

"Oh, it's Michael. Hang on, I'd better get it and let him know we're making progress."

Jen quickly filled him in on the conversations they'd had so far and mentioned that even Mrs. Grover had some great ideas which she was sure would make the event a success.

"Thanks, Mom," Michael said slowly, and Jen noticed a familiar hesitation in her son's voice. The one that was always there when there was something he had to tell her

—but didn't want to. She couldn't imagine what it could be.

"Mom?"

"Yes, Michael?" Jen waited, not knowing how to get him over the hump of saying what he needed to say.

"Um, I know that we—I—asked you to help with the shower. Amber was so excited, then crushed at every turn. I didn't want to have the shower like the wedding."

"Well, actually, she didn't know what happened at the wedding. We managed to keep that from her, remember? In fact, at the reception, she went on and on about what a wonderful job Greta had done."

"I know, Mom. I remember," Michael said with a groan.

"And Greta didn't correct her, either. Just sat there with everybody gushing about the whole thing."

"I know, Mom," Michael repeated.

"Not that I'm a bit resentful," Jen said, wishing she could have put all that back in her mouth. But it was true, after all. And this shower would be so much better since they could start from the beginning, not after the fact. And she told Michael so.

"About that..." Michael said, and hesitated yet again.

"What is it?"

"Uh, we had dinner with Greta over the weekend and—well—she's really excited about the shower, too. And Amber's excited to have it there."

Jen was silent for a moment. This certainly threw a monkey wrench into her plans. But she didn't want say that. Yet.

"So, okay, if Greta wants to have it at her house, how am I supposed to be helpful? If she says again she's got everything covered? And doesn't?"

Michael sighed and moved on to his fallback position. "Mom, it's girl stuff. How am I supposed to know?"

Jen was stunned. She hadn't imagined that Greta would have any interest in helping after she'd already dropped the ball. And certainly not that she'd want to still have the party at her own home.

She wasn't even sure what to say to her son. But apparently, she'd repeated enough of the conversation that by the time she hung up, Carrie and Mrs. Grover stared at her in silence, their faces sympathetic.

"I'm sure that won't be easy," Mrs. Grover said.

Jen sighed and looked down at her hands, her mind whirling with thoughts of how best to approach Greta to coordinate yet maintain complete control. Almost without her knowing.

"I don't see how I can," she said finally.

Carrie looked equally shocked. "I—I don't know if we can pull off a repeat of the wedding. How does that even work? With it at her house?"

Jen shook her head slowly. "I have no idea. I mean, I thought we had great ideas, and I was finally feeling like we could pull this whole thing off. It's only in a few weeks."

"I heard you say you were going to meet them tomorrow for lunch. Maybe you can just convince them that this is a better place to have it."

"Okay. You're right. I just want to have it here, and I

guess I sort of assumed that since she wasn't stepping up, we'd have full control. And not have to scramble like we did last time."

Carrie laughed and lifted her glass. "Well, at least we're lucky it's early in the day and she won't be needing a bartender. Not sure I want to try that again."

Faith nodded. "You were horrible at it. You're a much better dentist. Stick with that."

Jen was disappointed, but she spent the rest of the evening with her friends, trying to figure out how they could help Michael and Amber and still let Greta believe she was in charge. And she wasn't at all sure how to do it.

"You're meeting tomorrow?" Faith asked.

Jen leaned back in her deck chair and folded her arms across her chest. "Yes. I don't really want to but he sounded so—I don't know. Desperate."

Faith glanced over at the annex, where her workers would be returning in a couple of weeks. "I need to head inland anyway and pick up some fabric at my house for the new spring designs. The girls will be back and ready to start sewing again in a couple of weeks. Gene and I laid out a business plan, but it'll require more inventory."

Carrie, Faith—even Mrs. Grover—stopped with what they were doing and stared at Faith.

"Gene? Business plan?" Carrie asked. "I thought you were dating Gary."

"Who said anything about dating?" Faith asked, clearly annoyed. "I don't know what I'm doing. Gary and I—he's fun to go out with. He likes to go to cool places. Gene is a very successful businessman and has offered to help me with my business. You know, like a mentor."

"A mentor," Jen repeated. She'd seen how Gene looked at Faith when they were together, and she thought he was likely more interested in Faith than as a mentor. But he was very nice, and she was grateful that he was helping her friend get her business to even higher heights.

"Okay. You want to join us for lunch then? We can ride together."

Faith flashed both palms at Jen. "No. Not a chance. I can drop you off and head to my house, get what I need. You're going to try to change her mind, aren't you? I don't want to be anywhere near that."

Jen stuck her chin in the air in indignation. "What? So maybe it crossed my mind."

Carrie, Faith, and Mrs. Grover all laughed at the same time.

"I imagine you can be quite formidable, Jen. I don't blame Faith for wanting to just slow down the car and let you jump."

Jen couldn't help but laugh, too. Her friends, both new and old, sure did know her pretty well. And changing Greta's mind was exactly what she had planned. She just hoped it worked.

CHAPTER 3

Jen hadn't seen Joe for a few days, and she'd missed their quiet evenings alone when they'd cook together—before the flood. She hadn't had a kitchen since, so when Joe mentioned that his mother would be away for a few days, she jumped at the chance to make dinner for him at his house. They'd planned the menu together, and Jen laughed when he pulled his own apron out of the pantry and swung it over his head. It was one of the things that she'd fallen for first about him—and she loved when they cooked together. Tonight had been good therapy.

Jen and Joe finished up with the dishes, and she smiled as she took in the sight of the sparkling clean kitchen. She dried her hands on a dish towel and led Joe out to the porch. The night was chilly, but the porch was cozy, as it was heated. The bright stars shone in the night sky, and the peaceful sound of the waves crashing against the shore surrounded them.

"It was a fantastic dinner," Joe said as he sat down in one of the deck chairs.

Jen smiled. "Thanks," she said. "I'm glad you liked it. Couldn't have done it without you."

Over dinner, Jen had explained her plan to Joe. How she intended to convince Greta to let her host the shower at the beach house. That Greta had almost ruined the wedding. All of it. He'd been uncharacteristically quiet as she explained, and she took a quick glance at him to see if he'd been paying attention.

Joe looked out at the night sky for a moment and then turned to her. "Why do you feel like you need to do everything yourself?" he asked.

Jen sighed. She knew he was referring to the baby shower she was planning for Amber. She was determined to do it at her house so she could make sure everything went well. But she'd really had no intention of doing it all alone.

"Oh, I'm not doing it alone. Faith and Carrie are helping. Mrs. Grover even wants to help. And I'm sure your mother would—"

"That's not what I meant," he said, looking up at the stars. The wind picked up, and he reached for her hand and held it between his against the chill.

Jen looked up at Joe, puzzled. She wasn't sure what he was getting at. He had been so quiet during her explanation of her plan to host the baby shower, and she wanted to know what he was thinking.

"What do you mean?" she asked quietly, as the wind blew strands of hair across her face.

He turned his gaze back on her and gave her a warm smile. "You want to be able to control everything," he said, gently. "That's why you feel the need to do it all yourself."

She paused for a moment, surprised by his insight. She hadn't expected him to understand how she felt all her life since Allen died. But he did, and it gave her a sense of comfort and security that she hadn't known before.

"I guess I just don't want anything to go wrong," she admitted finally. "I mean, this baby shower is important...to Amber and everyone else who loves her."

Joe nodded in understanding, still holding her hand firmly in his own. He didn't say anything else, but the look on his face spoke volumes. It was more than that, though. She knew it, and she guessed Joe did, too.

"I don't know," she said. "I guess I'm just used to doing it all myself. Ever since Allen died, I've had to take care of everything. I raised two boys on my own, and I guess I don't trust anyone else to do a good job. Of anything."

Joe reached out and took her hand. "I wish I'd been there for you then," he said, and Jen's heart tugged at the sadness in his voice. "But I'm here for you now. You don't have to do it all."

Jen sighed and looked away as tears filled her eyes. She had been so strong for so long that it felt like a dam breaking now that she let herself admit what her life had been like. It was a relief.

Joe pulled her close and held her tightly, rubbing her back with one hand and stroking her hair with the other. It was almost as if he could feel the emotion she was feeling, and he wanted to make sure she knew that he was there for her, no matter what.

After a few minutes, Jen stepped back and wiped away the tears from her cheeks. She smiled up at Joe, feeling grateful for his understanding and acceptance.

"Thank you," she said softly, taking his hand in hers once more. "I know I'm not always easy to be around."

"No, you're not," Joe agreed, though his voice retained its gentle tone. "But I love you anyway. And I'm here for you every step of the way."

Jen smiled wider at this realization. She loved Joe—there were no two ways about it. And she wanted to believe that he was there to stay. She really did. But sometimes those old demons got the better of her. Better to just keep going. Hope for the best, prepare for the worst.

Jen seemed to sense what he was thinking and shook her head slightly before speaking again. "It wasn't your fault," she said firmly. "You were dealing with enough of your own grief without shouldering any extra burden. And you were married and had responsibilities of your own."

Joe nodded slowly in agreement before pulling her closer again.

She closed her eyes briefly against the night sky above

them. It felt good to have someone understand her like this--Joe had been here when Allen passed away.

Joe helped her on with her coat as she got ready to leave. "You know, you could leave the shower at her place, and you guys just do the rest, you know. You've got a lot of help for that with Faith and Carrie."

She sighed, not sure she could let go of the reins. It had been too long. Decades. And she knew she had a lot of help whenever she needed it—but it wasn't the same as being in control.

Joe walked her home, neither of them speaking but hand in hand. He walked her up to the door and left after a gentle kiss.

"Call me tomorrow and let me know how it goes with Greta. I hope you get what you want," he said as he headed back down the boardwalk toward his house.

For a moment, she considered that maybe he was right. She didn't have to be in charge. She could let her friends help, and she would be able to relax and enjoy the event. She took a deep breath and smiled, feeling a little more hopeful.

CHAPTER 4

Jen didn't say much on the drive to Michael and Amber's, playing over her conversation with Joe the night before. Maybe she should be able to just give this up, but it didn't take long for her to admit to herself that she didn't want to.

She arrived at Michael and Amber's apartment, feeling nervous but also excited. She had a mission—to convince Greta to let her host the baby shower at the beach house.

Faith dropped her off at the curb, declining to even come in and say hello. "Not a chance. If I get too close, you'll talk me into staying. I'll come in and say hello after it's all over."

"Oh, come on. You could help."

Faith shook her head as Jen got out of the car. "You don't need my help. If I thought you did, I'd stay. Good luck! May the best woman win."

Faith drove away with a wave, and Jen stood on the

grass outside Michael and Amber's apartment building, looking up at their second-story windows.

She took a deep breath and started up the steep, narrow stairs to Michael and Amber's apartment. Jen's heart raced as she stepped up, the old wood creaking beneath her feet. It seemed too dangerous for a new baby.

At the top of the stairs, Amber opened the door and welcomed them in with a smile. The apartment was tiny and cramped, barely fitting the four of them. Amber was glowing with happiness, her pregnancy obvious. She couldn't wait to have the baby shower, and Jen could see the hope in her eyes as she asked Greta and Jen to plan it.

"Jen! You made it!" Amber exclaimed, giving her a hug.

"Of course, I wouldn't miss this for the world," Jen replied with a smile.

Greta approached her, looking uncertain. "Jen, it's so good to see you. How are you?"

"I'm doing well, thank you. How about you? How's the planning going for the baby shower?" Jen asked, trying to steer the conversation towards her goal.

Greta's face fell. "It's not going as well as I had hoped. I just can't seem to find the right venue. Everything is either too expensive or too far away. And I'm not positive that my house would be big enough, honestly."

This was the first that Jen had heard that Greta was considering renting a venue—all the more reason for them to have it at the beach house. For free.

Jen took a deep breath and jumped in. "Well, I have a solution for that. I was thinking, why don't we have the baby shower at my house by the beach? It would be the perfect setting for a baby shower," she said with a warm—and encouraging—smile. "And it wouldn't cost a thing."

Greta looked hesitant. "But what about the kitchen remodel? Won't it be a mess?"

"The contractors promised me that they could be finished in time. Plus, I have plenty of room for all the baby supplies," Jen added, trying to sound as convincing as possible while she looked around the tiny, cramped apartment.

Michael stepped in. "Mom, I think it's a great idea. Your house would be perfect for the baby shower, and I'm sure everyone would love it."

Amber nodded in agreement. "Yes, it would be so much more relaxed at Jen's house. Plus, the views are amazing."

Greta looked back and forth between her daughter, her son-in-law, and Jen. She let out a sigh. "Okay, let's do it. We'll have the baby shower at Jen's house."

Jen felt a wave of relief wash over her. She had been worried about hurting Greta's feelings, but it seemed like everything might work out in the end.

Amber suggested they eat lunch, and Jen followed her to the kitchen, which was really just a corner of the living room. Greta sat and chatted with Michael as Jen helped Amber set the table and dress the beautiful salad she had made for them all.

As she set the last fork on the table, Amber surprised Jen with a hug. Amber whispered, "Thank you, Jen. I really want the shower to be awesome. And I know it will if you're in charge."

Jen was so surprised that she took a step back, wondering how much Amber actually did know about the wedding. They'd never discussed it, and Jen had no intention of doing so now. She really was a sweet girl, and Jen was happy that she could help—that's all that mattered.

As they all sat down to enjoy their lunch, the conversation turned to the excitement of the new baby. Jen couldn't help but feel grateful for the new life that was about to enter the world and for the opportunity to host the baby shower at her house, continuing on with a new generation. Just as she had planned.

As they ate, Amber started gushing about the baby shower. She talked about decorations and food and games, her enthusiasm contagious. Jen couldn't help but smile as she listened.

After lunch, Faith knocked on the door to take Jen back to the beach. Jen smiled as Faith hugged Amber and Michael and nodded to Greta.

"Oh, little darling, you look like you're going to pop. We'd better get this shower together fast," Faith said as she smiled at Amber.

"That's the plan," Jen said as she gathered her purse and sweater.

"Oh?" Faith asked, her eyebrows raised as she looked at Jen.

Michael hugged Faith and headed toward the door. "Yes. Greta and Mom decided to have the shower at the beach house. It's all set," he said with a big smile and nod toward Jen.

When Michael closed the door behind them, Jen hurried down the stairs and hopped in Faith's car. As soon as Faith got in, she put her hand up for a high five. Faith laughed and smacked Jen's hand.

"Mission accomplished," Jen said as Faith pulled away from the curb.

CHAPTER 5

Jen sat on the deck, her feet on the coffee table as she chewed on the eraser of her pencil and stared at the legal pad that hadn't left her hand in days. Ever since they'd agreed to have the shower at her house, she'd gone into overdrive trying to make sure they had everything in order.

Keith and Earl had stared at her, wide-eyed, when she'd told them they had a new deadline. She thought Keith had maybe even gulped. But they said they'd do their best. And the result of the full-court press was more - more sawdust, more noise, more commotion.

So, she'd taken to spending most of her time up on the deck to stay out of the way. She caught some movement from the corner of her eye and peered over the balcony of the deck.

"I can't hear you," Jen said as she leaned over the railing. Mrs. Grover stood on the sidewalk, and Jen could tell that she was talking, but she couldn't hear a thing over the noise of the tile saw downstairs in her kitchen.

Mrs. Grover had her fingers in her ears as well, but her lips continued to move. Jen gave up trying to figure out what she was saying and motioned for her to come upstairs. She pointed towards the outside staircase, as there was no way Mrs. Grover was going to be able to get through the big mess that was Jen's living room and kitchen. But at least Keith and Earl had gotten the tile saw they needed—from their new friend, Gene—and so progress was being made. Nothing could really make Jen happier at the moment.

"When I left this morning, I said I would be by this afternoon," Mrs. Grover reminded Jen when she finally made it up the stairs.

Jen nodded and pulled out a chair for Mrs. Grover to sit in. She'd been waiting for her to come and hadn't known what time, but now that Mrs. Grover was here, Jen was happy to share her list of things that she was making notes about for the baby shower.

"It's fine," Jen said. "I'm glad that you could come. There's so much to do. I really don't know how I could get through it all without your help, and Faith and Carrie of course," Jen said.

Jen noticed that Mrs. Grover was carrying a flower. "Oh, this is lovely," Jen said, admiring the flower.

Mrs. Grover smiled. "It's from Earl. He's a sweetheart." Jen smiled and tapped her pencil on the table.

"That's pretty much a flower every day now, isn't it?"

Mrs. Grover looked down at the flower, but Jen noticed that her ears had turned a lovely shade of pink.

"He's just a very nice man," Mrs. Grover said finally.

Jen nodded and could tell Mrs. Grover didn't want to say anymore, so they began to chat about the baby shower. Mrs. Grover offered to help, but said that she hadn't been to a baby shower in probably over thirty years. She began to name some of the old-fashioned baby shower games, much different from the ones Jen was familiar with.

Just then, there was a loud crash from downstairs. Jen and Mrs. Grover rushed down the stairs to find Earl lying on the ground, motionless. Keith over him, looking panicked.

Mrs. Grover ran to Earl's side and put her hand to his neck to feel for a pulse. Jen was already on the phone calling 911. Earl's eyes fluttered open, and he tried to sit up, but gave up with a groan.

"Don't move, Earl," Mrs. Grover said soothingly, her fingers on his wrist. It took Jen a minute to remember that Mrs. Grover had been a nurse, and she let out a sigh of relief. At least there wasn't any blood, but Earl did seem in a lot of pain.

When it seemed that Earl was okay, Mrs. Grover asked what had happened. Keith explained that he had been helping out with the tile installation and had stepped back to admire his handiwork when he accidentally tripped over a cord and fell onto Earl, who was standing right behind him.

The paramedics arrived shortly afterward, and Mrs.

Grover shared with them the vital sign information she'd been able to glean. Jen huddled with Keith on the deck, waiting for some information.

With Mrs. Grover's agreement, she and the paramedics insisted that Earl be taken to the hospital, as he hadn't been conscious when they first found him.

"Better to get things checked out, Earl. You'll be home before you know it," Mrs. Grover said in a soothing voice.

Earl had clasped Mrs. Grover's hand when she first went to him, and it didn't appear he was willing to let go of it now as the paramedics got him on a stretcher and started toward the ambulance.

"Keith, you want to go with your father?" she asked, not taking her eyes off Earl.

"No, ma'am, you go ahead. I'll follow. Be right behind you. Doesn't look like he wants to let go," Keith replied.

The paramedics loaded Earl into the ambulance, and Jen followed, her heart heavy with worry.

At the hospital, the doctor examined Earl and determined that he was okay, but likely had a slight concussion and needed to stay off his bruised knee for a few weeks.

It wasn't until all the adrenaline had subsided and they'd gotten Earl into Keith's truck so he could take Earl home that the thought of the baby shower crept back into Jen's head. Her heart sank as she realized that work on her house would stop, and she would have to postpone the baby shower.

Jen drove Mrs. Grover home in silence, deep in

thought. When she arrived at Mrs. Grover's home, the older woman smiled and thanked her for the ride.

"It's been a long day," she said with a sigh. Jen nodded.

"It sure has." Mrs. Grover squeezed her hand. "But don't worry. I'm sure everything will work out for the baby shower. We'll figure something out." Jen thanked Mrs. Grover for her kindness and then drove back home. She knew Mrs. Grover was right. Even though things seemed impossible now, she was sure that she would find a way to make the baby shower special and perfect.

CHAPTER 6

Mrs. Grover pulled back the curtains to make sure that Keith was packing up for the day and would be heading home soon. She wanted to catch him before he left. She had worked all afternoon to make sure everything was perfect.

She grabbed the basket she had filled earlier, covering it with a kitchen towel to keep it warm. In no time, Mrs. Grover was standing on the sidewalk in front of Jen's, holding the basket of food. She had made it herself, a batch of her famous chicken pot pie, which she knew Earl would enjoy.

She heard a voice behind her and turned to see Mrs. Russo there with a basket of her own.

"Oh, hello," Mrs. Grover said, her voice warm and friendly. She was pleased to see her friend after not seeing her for a while. "I didn't know you were coming."

Mrs. Russo smiled. "I couldn't let you have all the fun,"

she said. "I thought Earl might appreciate some variety. I brought some of my famous lasagna."

Mrs. Grover nodded, but suddenly wasn't as pleased to see her friend. "That's very thoughtful," she said.

At that moment, Jen stepped out onto the sidewalk, passing Keith who was on his way back inside to gather more equipment. "What are you two doing here?" she asked with a hint of a smile in her voice.

Mrs. Grover and Mrs. Russo exchanged a glance. Mrs. Grover cleared her throat. "We brought some food for Earl," she said. "We thought it might help with his recovery."

"Right," Mrs. Russo added. "A good meal made with love is the best medicine."

Mrs. Grover looked away, pretending to admire Jen's grandmother's roses, which were just about to bloom, trying to change the subject as quickly as she could. "Your grandmother would be thrilled to see the roses in such fine shape, Jen."

Jen smiled. "That's very kind of you," she said. She looked at the two women. "Nice to see so many people concerned about Earl," she said.

Mrs. Grover and Mrs. Russo both smiled, but neither of them said anything. Mrs. Grover blushed a little and hoped this would be over soon.

After a moment, Jen spoke again. "Mrs. Grover," she said gently. "Do you mind that Mrs. Russo brought food, too?"

Mrs. Grover took a sharp breath and shook her head.

"Of course not," she said. "Why would I?" All she wanted to do was deliver a warm meal to an injured person, not get peppered with questions.

Mrs. Russo chuckled. "Hm," she said.

Mrs. Grover bit her lip. She thought she had done a good job of hiding her feelings, but she enjoyed Earl's attention and the flowers he brought almost daily—until his accident. She knew Jen had guessed her feelings for Earl, but she was too embarrassed to admit it. She hadn't realized it herself until she saw him unconscious and pale on the asphalt. She just hoped Mrs. Russo didn't know.

The three of them stood there for a moment, the rose buds swaying in the breeze, the winter sun shining on the ocean in the distance. Mrs. Grover felt like she should say something, but it was clear her friends already knew more than she wanted them to.

Finally, Mrs. Russo broke the silence.

"Well, I should be going," she said. "I'm sure Earl will appreciate the food." She handed Jen the basket of lasagna and Mrs. Grover could have sworn she saw her wink at Jen.

Mrs. Grover handed her basket to Jen. "Would you please make sure that Keith gets this to take to his father?"

"Sure, he will," Keith said as he came down the stairs with his last tool bag in hand. "And he'd be mighty grateful if there was a little left over for him, too." He grinned as he took the baskets of food from Jen and placed them in the truck. "There hasn't been much to eat around our house lately."

Mrs. Grover smiled. She enjoyed Keith's company as well as Earl's, and she knew that he loved and respected his father deeply. She liked that about him, and on the evenings she invited Earl over for dinner, either Keith came with him or Mrs. Grover sent food home for him with Earl. She enjoyed doing it.

"Of course there is," Mrs. Grover said. "You didn't think I'd forget about you, did you?"

Keith smiled and tilted his head in her direction. "You've been very good to us, Mrs. Grover. I swear, I loved my mom, but she couldn't boil water. She had a lot of good qualities, though. Let me see, she was good at... ah, I just loved her. Not sure what she was especially good at. I loved her though. Actually, she was perfect. But I swear, if we keep hanging around with you, we might get used to it."

Mrs. Grover laughed. Earl and Keith had unique mannerisms and a way of speaking, but she really enjoyed their big hearts and great senses of humor. "I'd be honored if you did," she said, before she realized how bold she sounded.

She glanced at Jen, who was actually smiling now as she raised her eyebrows and looked from Keith to Mrs. Grover and back.

Mrs. Grover stood on the sidewalk with Jen until Keith rounded the corner, then she quickly went back to her house. She shut the door behind her, smiling to herself as she realized that she wouldn't be able to deny her feelings for Earl much longer. And she wasn't sorry. Maybe it was about time.

CHAPTER 7

Jen had barely slept a wink, running different scenarios through her head. Maybe she could finish the floor herself. Maybe if they all got together and…Joe's words rang in her ears.

"It's either postpone or toss it back to Greta," he had said, almost as a challenge. After their previous conversation, she had thought a lot about the control she had tightly clasped after she had been suddenly widowed. And as much as it broke her heart, maybe she should just let it go. Give Greta the reins. After all, as Faith and Carrie had reminded her, they were still going to be doing lots of things for the shower.

On her way out the door for her morning walk on the beach, she stopped to talk to Keith, making one last attempt.

"So, Keith," she began, and he turned off the tile saw

and took off his safety glasses, wiping his forehead with his T-shirt.

"Yeah, Miss Jen?"

"How's your dad?"

"Oh, he's good. Well, sort of good. I mean, he's gotten a little ornery. Maybe he was always ornery, I don't know, but he sure seems more ornery now. But Mrs. Grover's cooking is mighty helpful."

Jen laughed. "I bet. I'd make something for him myself if I could."

Keith nodded and looked around. "Yes, ma'am. I'm sorry it's taking so long. We were really on a roll there for a little bit."

Jen was pretty positive what the answer was going to be, but she had to ask one last time. "I know. So there's no way we can do this by the shower now, right?"

"Uh, well, I could try, ma'am... well, maybe... uh, no. Not a chance," Keith finally said. "Not just because I'm working by myself, but we were hoping to light a fire under the hardware store, but that was dad's specialty, and since he's out of commission..." He looked as disappointed as Jen felt.

"Okay. Just thought I'd ask. Thank you for trying, Keith," she said as she headed out the door.

Outside on the crowded boardwalk, Jen couldn't understand how all these strangers could be going about their business, not realizing the mess at hand. But the sun still peeked over the horizon and the waves crashed against the shore. Just like any other day, as far as they were concerned.

She took a deep breath and inhaled the salty air, feeling energized and invigorated. Enough to call Greta, anyway, and tell her what had happened. And basically admit defeat.

She sighed and looked out at the horizon, wishing she didn't have to make the call. But she did.

Greta answered on the first ring, her voice bright and chipper. "Hello?" Greta said.

"Hi Greta, it's Jen. I'm sorry to call you so early, but I have some news about the baby shower," Jen said, her voice heavy with reluctance.

"Oh, okay. What is it?" Greta asked, her voice hushed and curious.

"Well, it's about Earl, one of our contractors. He was in an accident at the house. He's going to be fine, but it's just that I won't be able to have the shower at my house," Jen said, feeling a twinge of guilt. "There's no way it can be ready in time."

There was a long silence on the other end of the line.

"Greta, are you there?" Jen asked.

Greta finally spoke, her voice excited. "Yes, I'm here. This is great news! I can take over the shower and I'm so excited to do it."

Jen was taken aback. Greta had been so uninterested in the shower planning that Jen was shocked she was now so enthusiastic about it. Jen couldn't help but ask, "What changed? I thought you couldn't have it at your house. It's much too late to even hope to find someplace to rent."

"You know, I got to thinking that you and your friends were a big help for the wedding, and it would be nice if I could have the shower at my house. You know, make sure everything was taken care of. And I thought over the number of guests, and I really think it'll work out okay."

Jen shook her head, but knew she had no other option. "Okay, if you're sure. You can take over the shower and I'll take care of the smaller details like party games, gifts, and decorations."

"Great! I'm so excited," Greta said, her voice bubbling with enthusiasm.

Jen hung up, feeling a twinge of annoyance. She was stuck with the drudgery while Greta got the fun part. But maybe it was for the best. Greta had proven to be unreliable in the past, so all she could do was hope that things were different. Perhaps this was the best solution. And as Joe had said, maybe she didn't need to be in control of everything. Everybody loved Amber—what could go wrong?

Jen turned around and started walking back home, prepared to re-think everything. As she rounded the corner, Mrs. Grover stood on the sidewalk in front of her house.

Mrs. Grover beamed as she saw Jen. "Good morning, Jen! How's Earl doing?"

Jen smiled sadly. "He's doing okay. Keith said he's a little ornery, though."

Mrs. Grover shook her head. "That's terrible, poor Earl. Is there anything I can do to help?"

Jen sighed. "Actually, yes. I had to move the baby shower, so I'm stuck with the details now, and I could use some help."

Mrs. Grover's eyes lit up. "I'd love to help. I'm so excited to get to spend more time with him. I'm sure he just needs a few good meals and some company. Although my sister is coming to visit unexpectedly. Drat. But I'll do anything to help make sure he feels better soon."

Jen blinked a few times as she stared at Mrs. Grover. Were they speaking the same language? It seemed to Jen that Mrs. Grover wanted to take care of Earl, and Jen could have asked her to wash the car, and it would have ended up with Mrs. Grover taking care of Earl.

"You have a sister?" was the only part of that statement she could begin to tackle.

"Hm? Oh, yes, I do," Mrs. Grover said, hurrying back into her house, probably to start making arrangements for Earl too. "She'll be here in a few days. She's interesting, I will say. You'll see."

Jen walked back into the house and found Keith at the window, stifling a laugh. Jen smiled too and said, "Did you hear that?"

"Yes, ma'am, I did. And I honestly think she's right. Dad's always more ornery when he's hungry, and Mrs. Grover's been feeding us for a while now. I'm guessing he misses that. I guess I do, too. My dad, you know, he can be a handful."

"But..." Jen started, but she just sighed. "Never mind. It looks like you can take your dad over there and talk to Mrs. Grover about looking after him."

"Sounds great to me. Did Dad tell you she makes the best chicken pot pie this side of the Mississippi? This is great. You know, Dad can be a little ornery."

Jen laughed and shook her head. "Yes, I think he did. Or you did. Somebody did."

Jen headed up the stairs, relieved at least that Earl would be taken care of and might get around to finishing the remodel sometime this year.

CHAPTER 8

When Jen had called and asked if she could meet her and Faith for lunch, she knew something was probably up, but she wouldn't have guessed it was this. Carrie tried to follow along as best she could while Jen explained what had happened with the shower since they last spoke.

Jen prefaced the whole thing with the news that Earl had fallen and they had to go to the hospital, but he would be okay, and that Mrs. Grover and Mrs. Russo had brought food over pronto for both Keith and Earl.

"Okay, well, at least that's good. How did that go? I kind of got the impression that Mrs. Grover and Earl were an item. How did Mrs. Russo get in the mix?" Carrie asked.

Jen shook her head. "I guess Joe told her, and you know how much she likes to share food. Just in general. And they arrived together, and Mrs. Grover was a little unsettled, but swore that she and Earl weren't an item."

"So she says," Faith said. "I think we've all seen the flowers he brings her every day, and that smile she gives him."

"Yeah, and the lipstick seems to be just for him," Carrie added.

"Well, I have to take her at her word, but it was kind of cute," Jen said as the waitress brought her eggs Benedict.

Carrie and Faith smiled as Jen smelled her breakfast and closed her eyes with the first bite. "Good?" Faith asked.

"I'm so sick of bagels from the toaster and granola bars I could cry," Jen said. "And now it looks like I'm not going to have a kitchen even longer."

"Yeah, me too. And Earl's going to get home-cooked meals, it appears," Faith said, barely able to contain her own glee at the bacon the waitress had put in front of her. Carrie usually had yogurt for breakfast, so she was also excited to have an omelette, no matter how long it had been.

"Okay, so you're telling us that Greta was supposed to have the shower and then you talked her into letting you have it, and then Earl fell and now Greta is having it again?" Carrie asked, sipping her coffee, her eyebrows raised.

"Oh, dang, you're making me dizzy," Faith said. "That's quite a change from the other day after we left Michael and Amber's apartment."

Jen shook her head. "I know. It's kind of hard to keep up with."

"So where do things stand now, then?" Carrie asked

between bites of her hashed browns. She held her empty cup up for the waitress, who filled it in a flash. Carrie was surprised she was even following all this since she'd only had a chance to drink one cup of coffee before Jen had called.

Jen shrugged. "I guess everything is the same, except she said she'll do the food and the cake."

"Uh-huh," Faith said. "Will she really? She didn't for the wedding."

"I guess I really don't know, Jen said, sipping her coffee and narrowing her eyes. "But maybe it's a good thing."

Carrie frowned. This didn't sound like the Jen she'd known most of her life. "A good thing? To let her be in charge of something so big?"

"Yeah. Joe actually said that he thought maybe I was a bit...maybe a little..."

"Controlling?" Faith offered, laughing when Jen nudged her elbow.

"Maybe. A little," Jen said.

Faith reached for the strawberry jelly for her toast. "He knows as well as we do that you had no choice when Allen died. The kids were so little. It's natural to just have to take charge. You were on your own overnight."

Carrie watched as Jen frowned and grew quiet. The whole thing seemed so long ago and, at the same time, like last weekend. Carrie had slept on Jen's couch for the first week and was sure that Jen had been in shock for at least a year. She wasn't sure Jen remembered, so she never brought it up, but it had taken a lot of strength and fortitude to try to make a normal life for two little boys on her own, and if that had made her a little bit controlling, so be it. They all understood.

"Thanks. I appreciate the grace. But that was a long time ago, so maybe it's time for me to start practicing not being in charge. And I'm pretty sure Joe would like that too," Jen said quietly.

"Jen, everyone loves you just the way you are," Carrie said. "Don't make me sing that song."

Jen laughed and held up her palms. "No, please don't."

"Speaking of love," Jen said, turning to Faith. "What's happening with you and Gene? Or you and Gary?"

Faith's eyes flew open wide. "Love? Not even close with either one of them. We're all just friends. They're different and I'm having fun with both of them."

"Fair enough. Do they both know you're all friends?" Carrie asked, not at all sure that the two gentlemen in question felt the same way.

"It hasn't come up, to tell you the truth. Gary invited me over for dinner, and that'll be fun. And Gene and I are going to meet later. He's helping me with my business plan."

"Well, be sure to report back," Jen said with a smile and a wink at Carrie. "So, you guys mind going over the list of things we need to do for the shower one more time?"

Carrie rolled her eyes and, as the waitress came and cleared their empty plates, Carrie asked for one more cup of coffee.

CHAPTER 9

Mrs. Grover peered out the window the following day, having made arrangements with Keith to bring Earl to her house when he started work at Jen's. The butterflies in her stomach woke her before dawn, and she passed the time preparing a roast chicken for lunch and a pot roast for Earl and Keith to take home. She had never cooked this much in her life and wondered what had changed. Maybe she had just never had anyone to appreciate it as much as Earl and Keith did. Either way, Mrs. Grover eagerly anticipated his arrival, pacing in front of the window with frequent peeks through the curtains.

As the morning sun began to rise, Keith pulled up in front of Mrs. Grover's house with Earl in tow. He was struggling with a cane as he shuffled up the walk. Mrs. Grover rushed out to meet them, helping to carry some of Earl's things and getting him settled inside.

"Can't believe I'm stuck with this old cane," Earl grumbled.

"Now don't you worry, Earl," Mrs. Grover said as she steered him towards the armchair. "I made all your favorites for breakfast!" She scurried into the kitchen and came back out with a tray of breakfast treats.

As they sat around and ate their breakfast, with Keith taking a muffin or two to go, Mrs. Grover asked about Earl's knee. "It's still a little sore," Earl sighed, "but there's no way I'm going to let it stop me from a good game of Scrabble!"

Throughout the morning, Mrs. Grover checked on Earl's knee often and made sure he had everything he needed for comfort and healing. Despite his injury, she could tell that lunch at her house had been a great decision. Mrs. Grover loved the company and Earl didn't seem to mind it either.

Mrs. Grover and Earl were in the kitchen, cleaning up after the delicious lunch she had made. The smell of the roasted chicken wafted through the air, mixing with the scent of freshly baked bread. Earl insisted that they set up a chair for him in the kitchen so he could dry the dishes that Mrs. Grover had washed.

"Earl, you don't have to do that," she said, trying to stop him. "You just need to rest."

"You're not going to find me being useless, not for a second," he objected. "I may not be much of a cook, but I've mastered the art of doing dishes. And I aim to do that." Mrs. Grover felt a warmth in her chest as she watched Earl move in his chair, humming along to the music playing in the background.

The kitchen was filled with the sound of music as Mrs. Grover and Earl worked side by side doing dishes. The music was old and familiar, something they both seemed to enjoy. With a smile, Mrs. Grover joined in the song, singing along to the Four Freshmen, then Frank Sinatra. Earl smiled and snapped his fingers, clearly enjoying himself.

Mrs. Grover felt so content that she hardly noticed her age-worn hands working the dishrag around each plate and cup she washed. She chatted away with Earl as if they were lifelong friends, talking about their childhoods and sharing funny stories from their pasts.

"You have a beautiful house here," Earl commented, as he stacked the dishes on the counter. "It's so cozy and inviting."

Mrs. Grover blushed. "Thank you, Earl. It's been my home for many years now."

When they finished the dishes, Earl took Mrs. Grover's hand in his. She felt a wave of warmth wash over her as they stood there, holding hands in the middle of the kitchen, listening to the music.

"If my knee wasn't injured, I'd ask you to dance," Earl said with a twinkle in his eye. Mrs. Grover smiled and gave his hand a squeeze.

The day had been so pleasant that Mrs. Grover wanted to learn more about Earl. She asked him about his wife, and he spoke of her fondly. He asked Mrs. Grover about her husband, but she wasn't ready to talk about it. The subject made her uncomfortable.

Earl immediately apologized. "I'm sorry if I asked too much. I want to get to know you, and I'm patient. I won't rush you."

Mrs. Grover smiled at him reassuringly. "I know you won't, Earl. I am sorry I'm not ready to talk about it yet."

Just then, they heard a car door slam outside. Earl's son had arrived to take him home. Earl reluctantly headed out the door, but not before giving Mrs. Grover a hug and asking her to dinner again the following night. She gladly accepted.

As she watched them drive off, Mrs. Grover realized that she did want to tell Earl more. She wanted to share her life with him, and the thought made her smile.

Outside, the sun was setting and the beach was quiet. A cool breeze blew in from the ocean, carrying with it the scent of salt and seaweed. The night sky was clear and filled with stars.

Mrs. Grover glanced around her cozy beach house with a contented smile. She was happy and, for the first time in a long time, she felt hopeful.

CHAPTER 10

Jen wondered sometimes if Joe's mother just felt sorry for her because she couldn't cook at her own house, or if she truly loved cooking for other people this much. Mrs. Russo's joy in the kitchen was contagious, and being with her made Jen miss her grandmother all the more.

Mrs. Russo had invited her over once again. Between Mrs. Russo's fabulous Italian meals and spending another evening with Joe, it hadn't even crossed her mind to decline.

She'd even been lucky enough to help in the kitchen, and she'd been so many times that now she brought her own apron—or the one Nana left for her, actually. The three of them always had a good time, and tonight Jen was on salad and Joe was on garlic bread while Mrs. Russo finished up her Italian wedding soup.

"Joey, would you grab the cannoli?" Mrs. Russo said as they finished their soup.

"Oh, Mrs. Russo, I couldn't eat another bite. Really," Jen said. Mrs. Russo's Italian wedding soup, with its little meatballs and tiny pasta in a rich broth, was one of her favorites. She hadn't declined seconds when Joe offered.

She ate it anyway. The smooth custard and crispy outside were too good to pass up, too.

Jen and Joe did the dishes, and as they got ready to leave, Mrs. Russo handed Jen a brown paper bag.

"For Earl," she said before Jen could ask. "And Keith, too."

"Wow," Joe said as he helped Jen on with her coat. "They're two lucky guys. I wonder if Earl is glad he fell. Between you and Mrs. Grover, they've got it made." He kissed his mother on the cheek before he shrugged on his coat.

"I don't know if they feel lucky, but I would venture to guess that Mrs. Grover does," she said with a wink. "And I wish them both the best of luck. It's not everybody who finds love this late in life, but I'll tell you, I've never seen two people more smitten than those two. I wish them both the best."

"Oh," Jen said. "It crossed my mind when you brought lasagne that maybe you…"

"Me?" Mrs. Russo actually gasped. "Good grief, no. No self-respecting woman would get in between something as plain as the noses on their faces. It's quite sweet."

Jen nodded. "It really is," she said as she hugged Mrs.

Russo.

Jen and Joe said goodbye to Joe's mother and stepped out into the night. The moon was full, the air was cool, and the night breeze was light.

"Let me walk you home," said Joe as he held out his arm.

Jen smiled and took his arm. "That would be nice," she said.

They walked slowly down the beach, content just to be together. They'd fallen into such an easy, comfortable rhythm, and Jen could hardly remember what it was like before they were a couple. She sighed and rested her head on Joe's shoulder, hoping that him thinking she was a little controlling wasn't a deal-breaker.

As they passed by the beach house belonging to Jen's neighbor, they could hear Mrs. Grover and Earl singing and having a great time. They both laughed but tried to stay quiet. Mrs. Russo was right, they just belonged together.

Joe looked over to Jen and asked, "Do you think they'll get married?"

Jen hadn't really thought about it, but it would be the natural progression when two people were in love. "Maybe," she said. "Mrs. Grover has been alone for a long time. And the way her eyes light up when she sees him, and his when he sees her—it's just really something. I can't imagine they wouldn't."

Joe shrugged. "Earl hasn't been a widower all that long. And who knows how Keith would feel about it. Maybe it's different when there are kids involved."

Jen stopped and glanced into Mrs. Grover's window. She'd made dessert and was happily feeding Earl every bite. "Look at that," she said and she held her hand over her mouth so as not to catch their attention. Even though they'd first met Mrs. Grover when she'd been spying on them, she didn't want to be caught doing the same thing.

"Oh, man. They're goners," Joe said and tugged Jen toward her front steps. He walked her to the door and he laughed.

Things had been so crazy since she and Joe met up again after so many years. He didn't talk much about his divorce, and she hadn't asked. And he already knew all about her and Allen, since he'd been Allen's best friend. She'd fallen for Joe slow and steady, remembering all the things she liked about him when they were teenagers. But in all this time, she hadn't once thought about getting married. Sure, she'd teased Carrie about it, but it wasn't something that regularly crossed her mind. And she had no idea how Joe felt about it.

She looked up at Joe and asked, "Have you ever wanted to get married again?"

Joe paused for a beat and then said, "Yes, I have, actually."

Jen smiled but said nothing. She wasn't sure what she'd say if he'd asked her the same and was glad he didn't.

But she was glad when he leaned in and kissed her goodnight, his warm hand on her cheek. Marriage hadn't crossed her mind, but this was a soothing reminder of the peace that comes with being in love. And Jen knew she had that with Joe. And certainly, marriage wasn't something she even needed to think about.

"I'm going to head back," he said. "I'm tired and have to work at the gondolas tomorrow. You good?"

"Of course. I'm going to hit the hay too. Carrie and Faith and I are finishing up the baby shower favors tomorrow. It'll be nice to get that done. Well, Carrie and I are for sure. I'll have to leave a note for Faith. She's on a date with Gary tonight."

"Oh?" Joe asked, his eyebrows raised. "That's still going on?"

Jen nodded. "Apparently. She doesn't say too much, but I don't know—I hope she knows what she's doing."

"She does. She's smart. But I have to say, I think I'm on Team Gene."

Faith laughed and said, "Me too."

Joe headed down the stairs and slipped out the gate.

"Hopefully Frank Sinatra doesn't keep you up," he said, pointing his thumb next door and wiggling his eyebrows.

Jen laughed and watched as he walked away. She smiled again as she glanced at Mrs. Grover and Earl through the window, happy that they'd found each other and marveling at how easy it would have been for them not to. It was just a coincidence that Keith and Earl had shown up on her doorstep, offering to fix her obviously leaking roof. And the rest was history.

At least she hoped it was, and that they were able to see what everybody else clearly did.

CHAPTER 11

Faith finally arrived at Gary's house after getting lost on the way. She had put his address on her phone, but in this neighborhood—up on Spyglass Hill—many of the houses didn't have numbers on the curb. She finally found it and slowly pulled up the long brick driveway, glad she didn't have to park her old clunker on the street. It might have gotten towed in this part of town.

"So glad you're here," Gary said as he opened the door. "I've been preparing all day."

He took her coat and purse and took her on a brief tour of the house. Faith couldn't remember when she'd been in one this nice—at least not someone she knew. The home tour had been in this area, and the houses this lovely, but she was just touring.

"Come this way. I have something you'll love to see." In his study, pictures of him all over the world lined the walls.

Him at Machu Picchu, in front of the Taj Mahal, the Sphinx. Her breath caught in her throat at the last picture she noticed—him under the Northern Lights. She'd always wanted to travel, but that was one of the places she'd wanted to visit most. She could imagine the cold, the dark sky, and the wavy rivers of light over her head.

But she couldn't imagine being all these places. As he showed them to her, he also had trinkets he'd brought from each place. By the time he was done, he'd taken the last sip from his very tall glass and said, "Oh, let's go into the kitchen. You must be wanting a drink by now, and I need a refill."

It actually hadn't crossed her mind at all, but she followed him into his huge kitchen, with beautiful cherry wood cabinets and a unique colored granite. She brushed her hand over it, thinking she'd never seen it anywhere before. The mint green and aqua blue swirls with burnt orange lines were mesmerizing, the way she imagined the northern lights would be. Jen would be so jealous she'd probably be speechless.

"Interesting, isn't it? I had it imported from Brazil. Van Gogh granite, it's called. The best in the world. In fact, I had to commission the plane and fly it home myself. And the contractors had never seen anything like it."

He handed her a glass of red wine while he poured himself another drink—something with a lot of vodka in it. "The red wine will go perfectly with the filet mignon I'm preparing. I made the balsamic reduction myself, as well as the mashed potatoes."

It smelled good anyway, and she smiled after she'd taken a sip of her wine. It was good, too—way upscale from what she and Jen and Carrie usually drank.

"Dinner won't be ready for a bit. Let me show you the rest of the house," he said, reaching for her hand and pulling her out toward what she suspected was the living room.

She caught her breath when they entered the room. The floor-to-ceiling windows looked out over the ocean, and down the hill to the harbor. The view was spectacular, and Faith asked if he knew where Jen's house was.

"Yes, it's right about there," he said, pointing a bit to the south. "See the Pavilion there? That should give you your bearings."

"Oh, yes," she said, and she thought they could probably see his house high on the hill from their house, too.

"I mostly like to look at the planes," he said, his smile fading. "We're so close to John Wayne Airport, and now that I don't fly anymore—well, I just like to watch them land and take off."

"It must be strange to be retired and not fly those big jets anymore. You must have loved it."

He hadn't mentioned his job since the first time they met, but he did talk frequently about how much he liked to fly. He turned to her and had an odd look on his face, something she couldn't quite read.

"Yes. Yes, I did."

She wasn't quite sure what to say as he fell silent, but she gave it a shot. "The view is just captivating," she said, pointing at the colorful boats bobbing in the water below. "It's like a living painting."

He was still quiet when a timer chimed from the kitchen. He smiled and hopped up from his chair. "Sounds like it's time to eat."

She followed him into the kitchen where he took some beautifully charred steaks from the oven and plated them with asparagus that had also been in the oven and mashed potatoes from a casserole dish.

He beckoned her to follow him into the dining room, and he pulled out her seat for her after he'd set the plates down.

"Everything looks delicious," she said, admiring how he'd pulled this all together. He opened a bottle of wine and poured her another glass, and one for himself.

"Good, I believe it will be," he said as he sat down and set his napkin in his lap.

"Thank you," she said as she cut into her steak. She blinked at it a few times—it was much more bloody than she was used to. She didn't want to make a fuss, but he must have noticed her expression.

"What is it?" he asked, his fork in mid-air.

She took a deep breath and said, "I—I don't usually eat meat this rare. All this blood. I like it a little more well-done."

He looked up at her, surprise registering on his face. "Nonsense. This is how filet mignon must be cooked. It's this way at all the five-star hotels around the world."

Faith hadn't been to many—any—five-star hotels, but it

didn't change how she felt about meat that wasn't well-done. She decided to just eat around the edges, though, where it was a little more cooked, and he nodded in satisfaction when she did.

They chatted over dinner—or he did, and she was happy to ask him about more places he'd visited. Time passed quickly, and before she knew it, he was carrying their plates into the kitchen. He didn't seem to notice that she'd only eaten a little bit of her steak.

He filled her wine glass again, and she thought she'd object because she had to drive home, but she let him fill it anyway. She didn't have to drink it if she felt like she shouldn't, and she wasn't going to stay much longer, anyway.

He offered her a seat in the living room and brought out a plate of Fig Newtons.

"Would you like one?" he asked.

Faith shook her head and patted her stomach as she gazed at the lights that had come up on the harbor below as night had fallen. "Oh, no, thank you. I'm stuffed."

Gary seemed taken aback by her refusal and he seemed almost offended. "Oh, come on. Just one won't hurt."

She shook her head again, politely declining. "No, really, thank you."

He frowned. "You don't like Fig Newtons?"

Her eyes widened. "Yes, I do like Fig Newtons. I just am so full that I couldn't possibly eat one right now."

He plopped down in his chair and put the plate of cookies down on the coffee table and drained his glass. "Is it just my Fig Newtons that you don't like? Why won't you take one?"

She stared at him and blinked a few times, unsure what to say. She'd eaten as much of the steak as she could stomach, but she really didn't want a cookie too.

"I need a refill," he said, heading toward the kitchen. She watched the lights until he came back, and when he sat, he stared at her for a few moments before he said, "Now, Faith, don't hurt my feelings. Fig Newtons are great. They're my favorite. I have them every night after dinner. Take one."

She felt her cheeks flush at the awkwardness of the situation, and eventually, she relented. She took one and smiled, taking a nibble and wishing she could stuff it under her seat cushions.

He smiled as she took one of the cookies, looking pleased that she had accepted.

Gary walked her to the door and kissed her goodbye. He seemed pleased with the evening and asked her to come back the following week. Faith smiled politely and agreed before leaving.

As the door closed behind her, she couldn't help but think about the strange evening. She had a lot to think about.

CHAPTER 12

"Thanks for coming to help, Faith," Jen said as she opened the door wide for Faith. "I wasn't sure you'd see the note, and I was so tired I just had to go to bed before you got home from your date."

Faith shrugged off her coat and nodded. "Saw it first thing. The only thing to look at in the kitchen, really, is the coffeemaker. Best place to leave a note."

"Well, I have a full kitchen here," Carrie teased. "Want me to show you where things are so you can make yourself something?"

Both Faith and Jen laughed. At least Carrie was self-aware and knew that she didn't want to cook—and was glad that her friends didn't mind.

"How was your date with—who was it? Gene or Gary?" Jen asked as they settled down to put together the favors for the baby shower. They'd agreed to an assembly line—

one of them cutting the ribbons, one of them tying the bows, and one of them filling the colored boxes.

"Oh, gosh," Faith said, pulling out another length of ribbon. "First off, I don't know if I'm dating either of them. I mean, technically, we're just hanging out and having fun. They're very different."

"That's an understatement," Carrie said, and she jumped when Jen kicked her under the table.

Faith didn't seem to notice. "I mean, Gene's one of the nicest people I've ever met. And he's been helping me with my business plan. He knows a lot about business. And he's very generous with his time. He feels like more of a mentor, maybe?"

"Well, he should be good at business. That makes sense."

Faith didn't seem to hear what Carrie had said, so Carrie just shrugged when Faith continued. "Gary, though —I don't know. We have a lot of fun.

"He knows so much about so many things, and he's been all over the world, as you know. He wants to take me, and you know I've always wanted to do that. And he seems comfortable anywhere. With anybody. Not shy, like me. He's a pretty big personality, you know?"

"Another understatement," Jen said, glancing at Carrie. Their eyes met, and Carrie was pretty certain she knew what Jen was thinking.

"What?" Faith asked, taking a break from thinking out loud.

"Oh, nothing," Jen said. "I was agreeing with you that

he's a pretty big personality. And he sure likes to have fun. I imagine there's never been a party he didn't like."

Carrie tried to hide her grin. "Probably not. He sure is making retirement look fun."

"Right," Faith said, smiling as she cut the last ribbon.

The thought crossed Carrie's mind to ask Faith if she realized that Gary was likely an alcoholic—having way, way too much fun, but she thought better of it. She changed the subject back to the shower, a topic that she knew Jen could talk about for hours.

Eventually, Faith cut the last of the ribbon and asked, "You guys mind if I head out? I told Gene I'd meet him for coffee."

"No problem," Jen said. "Oh, are you available tomorrow morning to pick up Mrs. Grover's sister from the airport? I have an appointment to taste cakes for the shower, and Carrie said she'd go with me. I'm not positive we'll be done in time.

Faith nodded as she pulled her coat on. "Sure, no problem. Text me what time."

She'd almost gotten to the door when she turned and asked, "Mrs. Grover has a sister? And she's coming here?"

Jen shrugged and nodded. "Apparently. Mrs. Grover said that she didn't want to leave Earl alone. And that she hadn't seen her sister in years, and this all came out of the blue. She also gave me an interesting description of her. I'll text you that, too. I'm guessing you won't be able to miss her."

Carrie waited a bit before she asked Jen, "What do you think of all that? The Gary and Gene thing?"

Jen shook her head. "I had to bite my tongue not to ask her if she's aware that Gary's an alcoholic. Fun, yes, but also a little over the top."

"So did I," Carrie said. "I wanted to ask, too. You think she knows?"

Jen shrugged again. "I don't know. If she doesn't now, she will eventually. She's got a really good head on her shoulders. And as you remember, her husband was—not fun at all, and the divorce was awful. It's been a while, and it's nice to see her having fun at all, really. She'll know what's right for her. And who are we to say, anyway?"

They fell silent for a while, each in their own thoughts. But they eventually put the finishing touches on the baby shower favors, making sure each one was perfect. Carrie held up a tiny ceramic teddy bear, painted a cheerful yellow, with a tiny pink bow around its neck.

"There," she said. "That's the last one."

Jen smiled and said, "It looks great. I'm sure Amber will love them. Thanks for all your help."

Carrie patted the bow she'd just tied. "I guess I got pretty good at it with the Christmas gifts for the Driftwood girls."

Jen nodded. "I guess I did, too. We all did. That was really something."

She glanced around the room. She'd been so focused on the favors that she hadn't taken the time to do it when she first got there, and Carrie watched the surprise creep across her face.

"You…have a Christmas tree. And it's still up in, um, January. Almost February."

Carrie laughed and loaded the boxes onto the kitchen counter. "Yep. You know how I feel about Christmas trees, but the girls wanted one so badly, I couldn't say no. And they don't want to take it down, either. I told them they're risking it going up like a dry tree in the forest. Which it is exactly like, except it's in the house."

Carrie had never had a Christmas tree before. This was a different Carrie—and Jen had noticed. She looked around the rest of the room, her eyebrows raised.

"And there are other things here that look a little unusual," Jen said, pointing to the men's shoes and hat sitting by the sofa and the bag of books at the bottom of the stairs, noting the signs that Dirk spent a lot of time at Carrie's house. "It looks like you have a family here," she said.

Carrie laughed. "Yes," she said. "I guess I do. He spends most of his time here, and Bethany has been over more and more. Especially now that Abby comes over a lot."

Jen paused. "Carrie…are you and Dirk going to get married?"

Carrie laughed again. "Not that I'm aware of," she said. "We kind of already are, I guess."

Jen looked out the sliding glass door to the waves crashing on the beach. "It was so, so sweet for him to ask you to go steady."

"Uh-huh," Carrie said, narrowing her eyes as she looked at Jen. "What about you and Joe? What's going on there?"

In fact, Jen's thoughts had drifted to her own relationship. She sighed and looked at Carrie.

"We had a wonderful night on the gondola. And actually, every night with him has been magical. To me, anyway. But I worry that Joe is just looking after me because of Allen. I mean, things have been going awful fast for us."

Carrie shook her head. "That's ridiculous," she said. "He loves you. This isn't fast."

Jen looked at her in surprise. "What do you mean?"

Carrie quickly caught herself, remembering her promise to Joe all those years ago when they were teenagers. Instead, she just smiled and said, "I think you should talk to him about it."

Jen was still pensive, but Carrie could see the wheels turning in her head. She knew this was something Jen needed to work out for herself.

They carefully placed the favors in Jen's car, and Carrie asked Jen if she was going to talk to Joe. Jen shrugged and said, "I don't know. I'm just not sure if he's really serious about it. Maybe he's just taking care of me because I'm a widow. The widow of his best friend, no less. I know he wants to help me, but…"

Carrie gave her a hug and said, "Jen, I imagine it would be easy to think that. I mean, it was complicated. But it was a very long time ago. That doesn't mean you can't move on and be happy. Joe loves you, and he's not just looking out for you. Talk to him and see what happens."

Jen smiled and nodded. They said their goodbyes, and Jen left, pulling away slowly to drive the few short blocks to her own home.

Carrie watched her go, feeling a little sad but also happy that Jen was willing to take a chance. Or at least thinking about being willing.

Carrie went back inside her beachfront house and looked around the room. She smiled, feeling the love and warmth that came from the slightly messy house. She thought of Dirk and their teenage daughters and said to herself, "Yes, I guess I do have a family here."

CHAPTER 13

The sun beamed down on the small airport as Faith checked her watch for what seemed like the tenth time. She had been driving around the airport for what felt like an eternity, waiting for Mrs. Grover's sister to emerge from the baggage claim area.

She had been told that Mitzie would wear an orange hat. She had also heard that Mitzie was a flamboyant seventy-something divorcee with five marriages under her belt, but she still wasn't prepared for the sight of her when she stepped out of the terminal.

Mitzie had on a bright yellow dress with a matching hat and a pair of large red sunglasses. Her hair was dyed the same red color, and she had a white bag with her that was almost as big as she was. She had a big, boisterous laugh that echoed off the walls of the airport. She had apparently met several male friends on the plane, all of whom wanted a hug goodbye.

Faith got out of her car, a little overwhelmed by the spectacle she had just witnessed. She nervously approached Mitzie, who, upon seeing Faith, erupted in a fit of hellos.

"Oh, my goodness! You must be Faith! Let me look at you!" Mitzie exclaimed as she threw her arms around Faith and gave her a big hug, as if they'd been best friends their whole lives.

"It's so good to meet you," Faith replied, still taken aback by Mitzie's enthusiasm.

Mitzie stepped back and smiled broadly. "And it's good to meet you too! Now tell me all about this Earl and my sister."

Faith hesitated for a moment, not sure how much she should say. Finally, she gave Mitzie the short version: that they seemed very happy together and were always making each other laugh.

Mitzie tried again to pry a little more information out of Faith, but she was determined not to say any more. So the subject quickly turned to Faith herself, which wasn't what she had in mind either.

"So, you're one of the neighbor gals Althea mentioned? You got a beau or something?" she asked.

"Yes, I'm dating someone," Faith said, blushing slightly.

"Oh, come on, don't be embarrassed! I ain't gonna judge. Life's all about having fun, right? Don't drag yourself down with a marriage," Mitzie said with a wave of her hand.

It was clear that Mitzie was nothing like Mrs. Grover. Faith smiled to herself, not exactly sure how she felt about her. She'd be anxious to see what Jen and Carrie thought and to find out how two sisters could be such polar opposites.

Mitzie hopped into the car and immediately started talking again. She told Faith about her dating life and her five husbands. Mitzie made herself comfortable in the car, immediately launching into a story about her five husbands. Faith had to laugh at the absurdity of it all, but she couldn't deny the fact that Mitzie's life seemed like an adventure.

Mitzie continued talking as she popped a piece of gum into her mouth and chewed noisily. She talked about her love for travel, her latest boyfriends, and why she enjoyed living life on the edge.

The drive from the airport to Jen and Carrie's house passed quickly with Mitzie never ceasing in her chatter. Faith felt more and more drawn to Mitzie's magnetic personality; despite their differences, it was almost impossible not to like her.

"Are you the one who's dating a pilot? That must be fun," Mitzie said, finally slowing down a bit with her biography.

"Yeah, we do have a lot of fun together," Faith said.

Mitzie nodded and smiled. "That's what life's all about. Fun!"

Faith laughed as she turned onto Newport Peninsula.

Mitzie rolled down her window and grabbed her hat, sticking her head out the window as they crossed the bridge.

"Would you look at that?" she said, pointing to the bobbing boats docked in the harbor. "I haven't been here for years. Forgot how beautiful it is. I could get used to this. California is the place to be!"

Faith laughed again. "I'm glad you like it here." Mitzie nodded, still looking out the window. She started humming a tune and then broke into a song. Her voice was surprisingly good, and she sang with passion. Faith found herself smiling and bobbing her head to the music.

Mrs. Grover was standing outside when Faith pulled up to her house. Mitzie hopped out and ran toward her sister, wrapping her in a big hug that Faith thought might topple them both. Mrs. Grover got as big a greeting, if not bigger, than Faith had at the airport. Faith couldn't help but smile as she opened the trunk to unload Mitzie's luggage, handing one of the suitcases to Carrie, who had just rounded the corner.

"Great outfit," Carrie said as she glanced at Mitzie and Mrs. Grover and waved, without even a hint of amusement. Faith looked at Carrie's orange capris and green top--of course.

Jen stared in Mrs. Grover's direction as she came out to help. "Wow," she said, her eyebrows raised. "She's sure different than Mrs. Grover."

"You don't know the half of it," Faith said, laughing as

they headed toward Mrs. Grover's house to meet Mitzie and drop off the luggage. "I can't wait to see how all this turns out."

CHAPTER 14

Jen put the finishing touches on the charcuterie board she'd put together especially for the first Friday night happy hour she and her friends had since all of this nonsense began.

"Whew. It feels like it's been a year since we've all been together up here," Carrie said, leaning back in her deck chair and popping an olive in her mouth.

Faith did the same and took the glass of wine Carrie held out for her. "Sure has. This all looks great, Jen."

Jen spread some of the Stilton cheese and fig jam she'd bought at A Market on a slice of French baguette, popped it in her mouth, and leaned back with a sigh.

"It does, doesn't it? And I can't wait to get this all behind us and actually cook something in the kitchen. It's been ages."

"Should be soon enough," Carrie added, filling her plate with Greek olives and feta cheese.

Jen reached for the ever-present legal pad that she'd been keeping notes on and scanned it quickly. "As far as I see, we've accomplished everything on the list, short of buying the food and ordering the cake. And Greta's supposed to do that part."

"You seem remarkably calm about all that," Faith said. "I know I've been kind of busy lately, but everything seems under control. What do you know about Greta's end?"

Jen shrugged. "Nothing, really. Haven't talked to her. I've been working on my control issues," she said with a laugh.

She felt a little better about the whole shower, actually —at least on their end—but wasn't quite sure if Greta was going to step up to the plate. And after Joe's comments about her need to be in charge, she'd done her level best to let it go.

"Oh, was it the control freak comment from Joe that made such a remarkable change in our dear friend Jen?" Carrie said, not able to hide her grin.

Jen shot her friend a dirty look. "He didn't exactly say control freak, but yes, I'm trying to let it go. Been singing the song from Frozen in my mirror every morning. I think it's helped."

They all laughed, and Faith rolled her eyes. "I can vouch for that. I can hear her."

"Whatever it takes," Carrie said. "But seriously, we're on track, right? We got the favors done, got all the decorations, invitations went out. What are we forgetting?"

Jen ran her finger down the list. "Well, we got prizes for

six games, but we've only picked three. So I guess we have to do that. Mrs. Grover had a couple of cute ideas, but we need more."

Jen explained the games they'd already settled on, and they agreed to ask around to some other recent grandmas to see what they could come up with.

"Knocking off for the day, Miss Jen," Keith said from below the balcony. "Gotta pry my dad out of Mrs. Grover's house. It's getting harder every day, I swear. I mean, I know he's a fun guy and not so ornery these days with her cooking. Until it's time to pick him up, anyway. I even offer him Fudgesicles, and it doesn't work."

"Okay, Keith, see you tomorrow. Thanks for all your hard work," Jen said as they all three leaned against the railing to watch Keith pry out his dad from Mrs. Grover's capable hands.

As soon as he was out of earshot, Carrie said, "Who would have ever thought that first day we saw Mrs. Grover timidly peeking out the curtains that this would all be happening?"

Jen nodded. "I think it was that day you spent with her spying on the open house here that really got her out of her shell."

"That, and the fashion show that Mrs. Russo shamed her into modeling in with us. She hasn't been the same since," Faith added.

"Nope. She wears lipstick every day now." Carrie sighed. "The times, they are a-changing."

They watched as Keith helped his father limp to the car

while balancing a basket of food for dinner—for the both of them. Jen ventured to guess that Keith didn't mind all that much as Mrs. Grover was always sure to include him in supper inventory.

Jen snapped her fingers. "Oh, you guys, I invited Mrs. Grover and her sister over for happy hour. After Earl goes. I can't wait to meet her."

"Oh, boy," Faith said. "We're going to need more wine for that, I think. I have never seen two sisters be complete opposites like that. You saw what Mitzie was wearing, right? Mrs. Grover has just graduated to capris, like you said. They are night and day, that's for sure."

They stepped back from the railing after Mitzie and Mrs. Grover came out of the house, Mitzie carrying a bottle of wine and Mrs. Grover a covered dish.

"Hopefully, there's something hot in that dish," Jen mumbled. "I haven't been able to use an oven for happy hour in ages."

Her wish was granted when Mrs. Grover came up the steps and handed her a warm dish of none other than Jen's famous artichoke dip.

"Oh, bless you," Jen said, removing the foil and inhaling the cheesy, creamy goodness she hadn't had for ages.

Mrs. Grover laughed. "See, Mitzie, I told you they'd want artichoke dip."

Mitzie followed behind her sister, her dress this day equally colorful as the day before when she'd arrived from the airport.

"Great dress," Carrie said before introducing herself. "Orange is my favorite color."

Mitzie looked down at her dress and laughed. "Might as well light things up, I always say," Mitzie noted, introducing herself to Jen and Carrie.

"It's lovely to meet you. Pull up a deck chair and join us. We brought up another one to add to our foursome. Mrs. Grover has a permanent seat here on Friday nights," Jen said, smiling at Mrs. Grover.

Mrs. Grover blushed—something they'd all noticed was happening more and more frequently—and pulled over a chair for her sister. "Thank you. I don't think I've ever had such good friends before," she said as Carrie handed her and Mitzie a glass of wine.

"Look at my big sister. Boy, I hardly recognize her. Best friends, taking care of a man every day, cooking up a storm. Who are you anyway?" Mitzie said with a laugh, looking around at the girls to agree.

"Well, Mrs. Grover has definitely changed a lot," Carrie said. And she briefly caught Mitzie up on how they'd all met, including Mrs. Grover peeking out her window at them.

"Ah, that sounds more like the big sister I remember. Always watching the world from inside."

Jen's heart tugged a bit as Mrs. Grover looked down at her hands and twisted a napkin. She was pretty sure that she and Mitzie hadn't been best buddies when they were growing up, but she could be wrong.

"I mean after the event. When we were kids, my goodness, we were all over the place. We rode our bikes all over, ate apricots in the summer until we thought we'd burst. Mom could barely get us to come home for supper," she continued. "But then that all changed with the event."

Jen wasn't sure what 'the event' was, but she could tell from Mrs. Grover's face that she didn't want to talk about it. The least she could do for her friend was change the subject.

"Oh, that sounds so fun." Carrie hopped in before Jen had a chance. "So, how long are you staying? We've been getting ready for a big baby shower. I'm sure your sister told you."

Jen smiled at Carrie for being a good friend to Mrs. Grover, helping her out of what seemed an uncomfortable spot. And she lent a hand. And fortunately, for the rest of the evening, Mitzie steered clear, too.

CHAPTER 15

Jen stepped over the scattered tools and construction debris that had become the norm in her house. She shook her head, still amazed that her house had been in renovations for so long, and that it had caused so much consternation—and trouble.

Making her way to the makeshift kitchen, she put on the kettle and grabbed a mug from one of the few cupboards that weren't filled with supplies.

As she waited for the water to boil, Jen thought about the upcoming baby shower for her daughter-in-law Amber. She had been so excited to host the event in her newly renovated home, but after Earl's injury, she was resigned to the fact that her house would not be ready in time.

Just as the kettle was about to whistle, Jen's cell phone rang in the other room. She hurried to answer, expecting it to be Greta, as they'd agreed to chat about shower progress.

Before Jen could even say hello, Greta said, "Jen, I have some bad news," her voice oddly calm. "The pipes have burst in my kitchen and I won't be able to host the baby shower. Is there any way you can do it?"

Jen's eyebrows rose. She looked around her own kitchen, taking in the bare walls, the unfinished flooring, and the lack of appliances. She didn't see any way she could host the shower in her current state.

"Well, Greta, I—"

"I knew you'd understand, Jen. Thanks so much. I'll email the guest list so you guys know who to contact about the change of venue."

Jen blinked a few times and said, "But—"

"Oh, and I hadn't had time to deal with the food, but I did order the cake. Thanks, Jen. See you then!"

Jen listened as Greta hung up, and all she could do was stare at the phone.

Just then, the door opened and Carrie walked in.

"What happened?" Carrie asked, looking at Jen. "You look—I don't know, mad? Sad? Can't tell. What's going on?"

Jen shook her head in disbelief, still trying to process Greta's phone call. "I don't know," she said, hearing maybe a slight hint of panic in her own voice. "Greta just called and said she can't host the shower. Tossed the ball back in our court."

Carrie blinked herself as she glanced around the room.

"Um, that seems like a big ask. She—we—oh good grief. How could that happen?"

Jen bit her lip, still unsure if they could pull off such a feat in the time they had. But she knew they didn't have a choice.

"Well, I guess we might as well talk it through. I'll call Joe and Keith. Would you mind asking Dirk if he might help? I'm sure we're going to need as many hands on deck as we can get."

Carrie nodded. "Sure. I'll ask Dirk." She glanced at her watch. "In fact, I have to pick him up in fifteen minutes. I told him I'd go with him to Laguna to show a house, and I only said yes because he promised we could go to the Beach Shack for grilled cheese."

Jen mustered a smile. "You're easy. Would you mind bringing me one? I'd love something to eat that's warm."

"Sure, no problem," Carrie said. "Okay, you call those guys, and we'll meet back here. Say, a couple of hours?"

Jen nodded, her heart lifting a tiny bit as Carrie hopped in her convertible and pulled away from the curb.

As Jen watched Carrie leave, she couldn't help but feel a twinge of excitement. Maybe, just maybe, they could make the impossible happen. Jen took a deep breath and walked around her house, looking for any possible solutions to make the baby shower happen. Despite the chaos of the ongoing renovations, she was determined to make the event a success. She knew it wouldn't be easy, but with the help of her friends, she was ready to take on the challenge.

CHAPTER 16

Carrie honked her horn outside Dirk's house, a two-story craftsman with its own charm, tucked away in a cul-de-sac, albeit one of the most expensive on the peninsula. In that part of Newport, the tip of the peninsula, most houses had been torn down, and new ones built in their place. But he'd renovated this one on his own, and although he spent most of his time at Carrie's, his daughter had grown up there and spent every other weekend with him since he and her mom had divorced.

Dirk emerged from the house with a smile and a wave, and she couldn't help but feel a warmth inside her. In fact, she had to admit that her house had felt a little empty without him earlier that morning. He spent most of his time there with her, and that warmth told her she preferred it that way. And no one could have been more surprised than she was.

Dirk had invited her on a quick trip down the coast and promised her a grilled cheese from the Beach Shack after he'd finished his business. He was scheduled to show a house for the owners of the decades-old beachfront restaurant. He normally didn't take listings out of Newport, but he'd been friends with the family since he was a kid and wanted to help.

Carrie then told him about the new situation surrounding Amber's shower. That Greta had abandoned ship and while Jen, Carrie, and Faith had worked hard to get most things ready for the shower, Greta—true to form—could not host.

Dirk shook his head. "I haven't even been involved, and I have whiplash. It's hard to keep up with you girls."

Carrie laughed and agreed. "I know. But the fact is that Jen has to have a baby shower at her house in two weeks, but construction pretty much stopped with Earl out of commission. I was just there, and she's panic-stricken.

But then she had a thought. "Hey. Jen and I were talking about this before I left to pick you up. Keith's been working steadily, and the floor is finished. He's done a lot more than she thought he could on his own. The appliances and cabinets have arrived and are in the garage. Jen's the queen of painting, and as much as I hate to admit it, I've become a fairly solid assistant for her when she's on a roll. What if we try to pull this off?"

Dirk raised his eyebrows as Carrie turned her convertible down Pacific Coast Highway toward Laguna Beach.

"We? I'm not exactly an expert in construction."

Carrie smiled, remembering the time she and Dirk had tried to hang a picture at her house, and he'd hit his thumb with the hammer. And then they'd both dropped it, dissolving into laughter.

"Yeah, I know. But Keith said the other day that all the big things are done, as far as drywall, floor, that kind of stuff. Doesn't that just leave installing cabinets? And plugging in appliances?"

Dirk shrugged. "Again, I'm no expert, but I'm pretty sure it's not as easy as you're making it sound."

Carrie sighed. There had to be a way, even if it wasn't quite as simple as she thought.

"Didn't Keith also say that he was having trouble getting some things from the hardware store? And that Home Depot and Lowe's are out of some things, too? I remember that being part of the original decision, that they couldn't get it finished in time."

Carrie's eyes widened. "You're right, but doesn't Gene have something to do with the hardware store? I thought I remembered my mom mentioning that before Christmas."

"And he got Keith the tile saw. Maybe he can pull some strings," she said, feeling a little more excited about the prospect.

"Hm," Dirk said, looking out over the cliffs at the ocean. "I do remember that. And he's a really nice guy. I bet he would help if he could."

"I'll call him and ask him to meet us at Jen's in a couple

of hours. Between us and Joe and Keith, maybe we can make this happen."

"Oh, thank you! I'll call Jen and tell her we'll be there then and try not to panic in the meantime. I know it would mean a lot to her to finish up and be able to have the shower."

After a few minutes, Dirk ended his call and said, "Okay. He's all in. Or at least willing to survey the possibility."

Carrie smiled and would have kissed him if she hadn't been driving. "Great. Jen doesn't sound great, but she said Joe and Keith will be there too, and I heard maybe a tinge of hope."

Dirk seemed happy to rally the troops and help, and Carrie couldn't help but feel like he was part of the team. It was one thing she'd loved most about him when they'd first met—that he was so generous with his time and always willing to help.

The two of them arrived at the Beach Shack and got their grilled cheeses to go, now that they had to be back in Newport before too long. Carrie did eat hers while Dirk took her car and met the potential buyers. She'd barely had time to people-watch—the Beach Shack had the weirdest array of customers she'd ever seen, from surfers still in their wetsuits to men in business suits, when he pulled up to the curb at the park and whistled for her to hop in. She grabbed the trash and tossed it on her way and hopped.

As Dirk headed north back to Newport, she asked him how the showing went.

He shrugged and said, "Never know. Maybe good, maybe not, but the house sure is cute. It'd be a great spot for somebody."

Carrie nodded, and they spent the rest of the trip home speculating about their new project—finishing Jen's house.

CHAPTER 17

Jen had said little on the phone when she called, but Joe was as sure as the sky was blue that it had something to do with the shower. He'd never experienced so many plan changes, and since he did know that Jen was — he wished there was another word for controlling — probably having a challenge of some kind.

"Hey," Joe said, walking over to Jen and giving her a hug. "What's going on?"

The sight of her quickly confirmed his suspicions. Her face was drawn, and she looked like maybe she'd been crying — something he'd never known her to do. She explained Greta had shown her true colors again and bailed on the shower, and with time being so short, they were really in a bind.

But he knew how important this baby shower was to Jen, and he also knew how stressed she was about the construction. And now, both worries had collided into one. No wonder she was worried.

Joe took Jen's hand and squeezed it reassuringly. "We'll figure it out. Let's make a list of everything that needs to be done, and we'll take it from there."

Joe happily opened the door to let Keith in as soon as he knocked.

"I came as soon as I could. Another change?" Jen's laughter sounded like it could have quickly turned into a sob, and Joe wrapped his arm over her shoulder as she explained.

Keith sighed. "You say you've got help? No offense, Joe, but I'm not sure even the two of us could get it done on our own."

"None taken," Joe said with a smile. "Pretty sure we've got Carrie's boyfriend Dirk and Gene. Maybe with the four of us? They'll be here shortly."

"Gene?" Keith asked with a look of surprise. "The one who brought the tile saw blade?"

"I believe so, yes. The guy who's here every once in a while with Faith."

"Well, that might change things," he said, taking a small notepad from his pocket and a chewed-on pencil from behind his ear.

"It does?" Joe didn't know Gene very well, but he didn't look much stronger than he and Dirk were and couldn't imagine how he could change the entire equation.

"Yep. Sure does."

"How?" Jen asked quietly. "I mean, I know he's a nice guy, but—"

Keith stopped scribbling for a moment and held his hand up to Jen. "Gotta concentrate, Miss Jen. Gotta concentrate. You know, sometimes it takes a lot for me to do that, and this might be one of those times. Yessirree Bob."

Jen smiled, which for Joe was a good sign. Keith did have a way of lightening things up, and he and Jen followed him around as he looked in every nook and cranny, at every bundle of supplies down to the number of screws and took notes the entire time.

By the time they finished, the list was long.

"See, now we know what we're up against. I was waiting for the old man to come back, and there wasn't as much of a rush, but now we can see it right here. All on paper. And I think maybe we can pull this off."

He held up his tiny notepad — he'd written way more than one page full — so Joe and Jen could see. Joe couldn't quite make it all out, but he knew Keith had been pretty thorough. He'd watched him.

Joe breathed a sigh of relief. "That would be amazing, Keith. Thank you so much."

"Keith, I don't know what to say," Jen added, and Joe couldn't hold his laugh in at the look on Keith's face when she rushed over and gave him a big hug.

His face turned a deep red, and he looked up at the ceiling, his arms outstretched, waiting for Jen to let him go. Jen hadn't noticed and looked relieved, and Joe could see the tension melting away from her face. "Thank you so much, guys," she said, smiling. "I don't know what I would do without you."

Joe smiled back, feeling a warmth in his chest. He was happy to be able to help her, and he was sure they could get the job done.

"We're going to need to get right on this, Miss Jen. You said that Mr. Buchanan and Dirk were planning to meet us here?" Jen nodded. "That's what Carrie said."

"Well, let's just cut to the chase. Can you let them know to meet us at the hardware store? This is all going to hinge on getting the supplies we need. You know I've had trouble with that. But with Mr. Buchanan onboard, that should be a piece of cake."

Joe wasn't sure what Keith meant and shrugged when Jen glanced at him, looking as confused as he felt.

"Okay, I will," she said, looking around for her phone. She smiled when Joe retrieved it from the counter and handed it to her.

"Let's go, Joe," Keith said, motioning for Joe to follow him. "My truck can practically drive there by itself; it's gone so many times in my life. We have the list, and we can get a jump on things we need before they get there."

Joe shrugged again with a smile, and he gave Jen a gentle hug. As he pulled away, he could see her face relax. He smiled, knowing he had been able to help her and make her feel a little better. Certainly better than when he'd first come over.

As he walked to Keith's truck, Joe thought about how

lucky he was to have Jen in his life. He knew he'd do anything to keep her safe and make her happy, and he was glad he was able to do that — although he had a sneaking suspicion that this experience with Keith might be a little bumpy. Or interesting, at least.

CHAPTER 18

"I haven't spent much time in a hardware store," Dirk said to Joe when they met at the front door. "Have you?"

Joe stopped and looked at the sign. "No, not really. I mean, not since I was a kid. I used to come here with my dad, though, pretty much every weekend. Now it's pretty much Lowe's."

Dirk nodded. "Pretty much. The mom-and-pop stores aren't around much anymore, especially around here where everything's torn down for something newer, bigger, and better. But I do know this place has been here as long as I can remember."

Keith opened the door for both of them, but Joe didn't go in before saying, "Hey, you guys, I wanted to thank you for all of this. It's going to be some rough days ahead. Hopefully, not as many with some help."

Dirk nodded. "No problem, man. Happy to do it. Slow time at work for me anyway."

Keith opened the door and held it for them both. "It's my job, so no thanks necessary. But I'd probably do it for fun if it wasn't."

Joe laughed, believing every word of that. "Remind me to thank Gene when I see him."

"Okay, consider yourself reminded," Keith said as they approached the customer service desk.

Joe looked up and blinked a few times before he recognized Gene. They'd met more than once, but seeing him behind the counter had thrown him sideways. Joe was a little flustered and said, "I didn't know you worked here."

Keith laughed and slapped his knee. "Work here? Pshaw. Mr. Buchanan is the owner. Been in here most days I have. Don't see him much anymore, though. Nice to see you, Mr. Buchanan," Keith said, shaking his hand.

"Hello, Keith." Gene nodded and smiled. "Not own. Owned. Sold the business when my wife passed a while back."

"Oh," Keith said. "I'm sorry about that, Mr. Buchanan."

"Thank you, Keith," Gene said. "Long time ago. But nice to see you. How can I help you guys? Couldn't believe it when Dirk told me your timeline. Pretty big bite to chew, that."

Joe extended his hand and smiled at Gene, who smiled and nodded as Joe thanked him. "Yes, that hasn't been lost on us," Joe said with a laugh. "Hopefully, you've been spared from all the shower drama, and Faith hasn't talked about it as much as Carrie and Jen."

His eyes clouded for a moment. "No, she hasn't. I don't see Faith as much as I'd like to, to be honest." He cleared his throat and continued. "But it's my pleasure to be a part of it." He gestured around the store. "I don't own the place anymore, but everybody who works here was here when I was, and they are very kind when I need help."

"Easy to do, Mr. Buchanan," Keith said. "Thanks for helping out."

"My pleasure," Gene said. He held his hand out for the list Keith had made, and the two of them huddled for a moment, looking things up on the computer and taking a quick walk to the lumber aisle.

"I feel a little useless," Dirk said.

"Here, be useful. Drink this," Joe said, grabbing a Coke from the cooler by the cash register. "I don't think we're going to feel useless for long."

CHAPTER 19

Jen had to call an emergency happy hour with the turn of events, not at all sure how she was going to pull this off. The guys seemed pretty confident that they could finish in a week. Joe and Keith had said that with the addition of Gene and Dirk, and Gene's ability to grease the skids at the hardware store, it should be possible.

So now all that was left was to put more on her long-suffering friends. They might be surprised—except for Carrie—but Jen knew they wouldn't object, and that brought some comfort.

Faith and Carrie came up on the deck first, both laughing at her. Jen knew they would, and had reconciled herself to their teasing. But she knew they'd get past it.

"Oh, good grief, this has to be the longest, most drawn-out shower conversation in the history of humanity," Faith said when they met on the deck.

"Okay. So you got your wish, sounds like. The shower is here?" Carrie asked. "Dirk filled me in a little bit. I guess they're all pitching in to help. That's really nice. Gene, too."

Faith had been pulling a deck chair over and paused for a moment, glancing at Carrie. "He is?"

Carrie nodded. "Yeah, I guess he owns—or owned—the hardware store here in town. He can get the supplies that had been holding up Keith and Earl. Very nice of him."

Faith grabbed the deck chair and pulled it over to the table. "He does? You mean Buchanan Hardware, that's been there forever? How did I not know that?"

Carrie shrugged. "Yep, that's the one. And I have no idea how you guys could be friends and you wouldn't know that. You know everything there is to know about Gary, it seems."

Faith laughed. "Almost impossible not to. Gene doesn't talk about himself nearly as much as Gary does."

"No doubt about that," Jen said with a wink at Carrie, who rolled her eyes.

"Hm, okay. Should I ask Gary?" she asked as she sat down and reached for Jen's legal pad.

She stopped and looked up when both Jen and Carrie said, "No," at the same time.

She looked from one to the other and shrugged. "Okay, suit yourself."

She glanced at Jen's legal pad and flipped the top page to the second page of things they were supposed to be getting done.

Jen smiled and sat down herself. "Thanks for not

rubbing it in too badly. You have earned the right to say be careful what you wish for."

"Sounds like it," Mrs. Grover said as she and Mitzie came through the French doors onto the deck.

Jen gave them a quick rundown of what happened, about Greta's pipes and their agreement that Jen and the girls would now do food.

"Oh, wow," Carrie said slowly. "I can pick things up if you want to cater, but you know I'm not your wingman on this food part."

Faith laughed at Carrie's wingman reference. They all rotated that job, based on what was needed. "No, you're definitely not on deck for this one. But you can shop. I know that for a fact." She turned to Jen and handed her the list. "I see you've roughed out some menus. So you're not going to cater?"

Carrie nodded and looked relieved. "Oh, that could work. Lots of places to choose from. La Cerveza caters great burritos. XX also. Lots of choices."

Jen shook her head. "Okay. I know what you're all going to say. That I'm controlling. That it's ridiculously ambitious and finally, what am I thinking. I get it. But I really, really want to do something homemade. It'll be the first event in the house after the remodel and…well…it's our first grandbaby. I want Amber to have something special…"

"Like your Nana would have done." Faith finished her sentence as it was pretty clear what she wanted to say.

"Yeah, okay. Guilty as charged," Jen said.

Faith frowned. "Okay, but for that, we'd have to cook things in advance and just need to heat it up, right? I mean, we—we—haven't had to cook for that many people on the day of an event in a really long time. We need to have it ready. And your kitchen isn't going to be ready that much in advance."

Mrs. Grover had listened intently as they bounced around ideas. And Mitzie had uncharacteristically kept to herself during this discussion as well.

Mrs. Grover cleared her throat and said, "I have an idea. I've had a fair amount of practice cooking of late."

Mitzie popped in to add, "That's for sure."

Mrs. Grover looked over at Mitzie, who raised her eyebrows and mouthed, "What?"

"As I was saying, I've gotten quite proficient at cooking rather large quantities for Keith and Earl. It's been quite an experience. And since I send meals home with Keith, I have gobs and gobs of disposable aluminum baking pans."

All eyes turned in her direction, and as she spoke, Jen's smile widened. "Are you saying that you'd like to try doing this on our own? No catering?"

Mrs. Grover firmly nodded. "Absolutely. We can use my kitchen to cook and store the food as it's right next door, for one thing."

Carrie literally raised her hand and said, "We can store things at my house, too. I have a big refrigerator. And it's empty."

Jen laughed and agreed. "Of course it is. Like usual. Thank you!"

"Of course," Carrie said. "I can't cook, but I can open the refrigerator. And help in any other way."

Mrs. Grover smiled at Carrie and patted her knee. "There are lots of ways to help, my dear. We'll need plates, utensils, cups, napkins, all in the shower theme colors."

Carrie's face lit up. "I can do that. Definitely your wingman for that."

"Hm," Faith said with her eyes narrowed. "Maybe I'd better help you. Your sense of color may be be a little off."

Carrie looked down at her neon yellow print flowered dress, and Mitzie laughed.

"She's got the best taste of all of you," she said, brushing her bright red hair from her face with a smile.

"What is it, Mrs. Grover? You look like you want to say something," Carrie said.

Mrs. Grover had been quiet for a while and had shredded a napkin in her lap.

"Um, I have a favor to ask."

They waited while Mrs. Grover reached for another napkin, presumably to shred it too.

"Yes?" Jen asked slowly. "Earl has asked me to accompany him to his high school reunion here on the peninsula. And I was wondering if you all thought I should attend."

"Should you? Of course you should," Mitzie said before anybody else could say a word. "Why wouldn't you?"

"Mitzie, I know there's never been a party you wouldn't go to, but it's different for me. I haven't been anywhere like that in—oh my goodness, maybe half a century."

"Well, then, it's high time you go," Carrie said. She pulled Mrs. Grover up and stood next to her.

"We look like we could be the same size. I'll bring over a few gowns for you to try on. I have a ton from the stupid things my mother made me go to."

"Oh, would you?" Mrs. Grover said, sounding nervous. "That's one of the things I was worried about. I'm not a shopper."

"You don't have to be," Jen said. "Carrie can fix you up. And we can all come see. It'll be so exciting!"

Mrs. Grover looked around the deck, a tear rolling down her cheek. She dabbed it with a napkin and reached for Carrie's hand.

"I never thought I'd have such good friends. And next door, too. And my sister here? I am so blessed."

"We're the ones who are blessed," Faith said, standing and hugging Mrs. Grover.

"We all are," Jen said, wishing her grandmother was there to join in the hugs.

Jen looked around at her friends, and tears welled up as she set the list down on the table. "You guys, I know I'm a handful, but I truly, truly appreciate you supporting this. I know it's going to be a lot of work, but I am so grateful to be doing it with all of you."

"You're welcome," Faith said as she reached for Jen's list. "No time for hugs now, we've got a menu to plan. Oh, and games. We need more games."

Mitzie raised her hand like Carrie had. "I can do games. I've been to lots of parties, believe me. I'm on it."

Jen smiled as Mrs. Grover looked at her sister with an expression she couldn't quite make out—maybe apprehensive? But also grateful.

"Thank you, you guys. I don't know what to say," Jen said, her hands on her heart.

"Nothing to say, except what you want us all to make," Faith said. "We've got to get on it to make this happen. No time to waste."

Jen couldn't believe her friends were pitching in without even teasing her. Not badly, anyway. But she was fully prepared for that to come later—after the shower. For now, they were all on board.

CHAPTER 20

They'd all been working for days, from sunrise to sunset, and it was finally becoming apparent to Jen that they were going to finish just in the nick of time, with one day to spare. But it had been grueling, and she couldn't even imagine how she'd ever repay her friends for this—but she'd think of something.

Just about when Jen thought she'd painted the very last of the new drywall, Earl walked into the room.

"Earl!" she exclaimed. "You must be feeling better."

"I am, and the doctor agrees. I'm cleared to do—something. But it looks like there's not much here for me to do." He whistled as he looked around Jen's kitchen and living room. "Wow, you've all been hard at work."

"Yeah, and you've been sitting over at Mrs. Grover's playing Scrabble and eating all day," Keith teased.

His father feigned horror but laughed. "I guess you're

right. But I'd be the first to tell you all that you didn't need me one bit."

"Would you like to do the honors, Keith?" Joe asked after he and Dirk had slid the new stainless steel refrigerator almost all the way in between the new cabinets, now covered in beautiful white quartz.

"Aw, shucks," Keith said. "I didn't do nothing. I just—well, I guess I did do something." He bowed as he took the plug from Joe and leaned behind the refrigerator, plugging it in and closing his eyes when it began to hum.

"Oh, my gosh," Jen cried. "It sounds like angels in heaven!" She ran over to Keith and hugged him, and this time he smiled and hugged her back.

Jen, Joe, Carrie, Dirk, Faith, Gene, Earl, and Keith all stood in the middle of the remodeled beach house.

"Wow, guys, this is amazing!" Jen exclaimed as she looked around the room. "I can't believe we actually did it!"

"Yeah, we make a pretty good team," Joe said, putting his arm around Jen.

"Speak for yourself, I almost lost a thumb," Dirk grumbled, holding up his bandaged hand.

"Aw, come on Dirk, it was worth it for this beautiful kitchen," Carrie said, giving him a playful nudge.

"And let's not forget Gene's help," Jen added, looking at her friend. "Without you, we would have never been able to wrangle all the supplies we needed."

"Hey, what can I say? I know my way around a hardware store," Gene said with a grin. "Just call me the hardware wrangler."

Jen smiled as Faith walked over to Gene and gave him a hug.

"Couldn't have done it without Earl and Keith. They were the brains behind this operation," Joe said, gesturing to the two contractors.

"Yeah, Earl, who knew you had such a talent for tiling," Faith said, admiring the new tile floor.

"Well, I've been doing this for a long time, but I have to say, I'm pretty impressed with the work my son did here," Earl said, patting Keith on the back.

"Thanks, Pop, but I couldn't have done it without all of your help," Keith said, looking around the room.

"Okay, enough with the mutual admiration stuff," Faith said with a laugh. "So, what's next on the list?" she asked, looking around the kitchen.

"Well, we still have a little bit of clean-up to do before the shower," Jen said, biting her lip. "And then after the shower, of course, the fun part. Decorating."

"Oh boy, here we go again," Joe said with a laugh.

"Hey, I happen to be a pretty good decorator," Carrie said, sticking her tongue out at Joe. "I can help."

Silence fell over the room as all eyes turned to Carrie. "What?" she asked before they all burst into laughter.

"No," Jen and Faith said at the same time. Carrie rolled her eyes and looped her arm through Dirk's, smiling.

"And I'm obviously pretty good at holding things," Dirk said, holding up his bandaged hand.

"I know I'm on pillows," Faith said. "Gene and I have a

master business plan, and the girls'll be back to sew next week."

"Look out, world," Gene said. "Here comes Faith's pillows."

Jen smiled as Faith looped her arm in Gene's, and he looked at her with pride. And maybe a little something else. "Well, it looks like all we have left to do today is cleanup. Tomorrow, all the chairs get delivered, and we're ready, so we have a day to spare," Jen said, shaking her head in amazement.

"Okay, it looks like we have our team set then," Carrie said, clapping her hands together. "We're in the home stretch. The ninth inning. The last mile, and whatever else applies."

And with that, they sprang into action, cleaning up the remaining mess and putting the finishing touches on the kitchen. They laughed and joked as they worked, and Jen was relieved to have the anxiety they'd all felt for weeks lifted, and she knew it all would be worth the effort. Soon, they all collapsed into chairs on the deck, ready to watch the sunset.

"I have to say, I'm pretty impressed with what we were able to accomplish," Gene said, taking a sip of his beer that had been chilling in Jen's new refrigerator.

"Me too," Earl nodded in agreement. "I never thought this kitchen could look this good."

"Yeah, and it's all thanks to this incomparable group of friends," Jen said, smiling at everyone.

"Here, here!" Joe said, raising his beer in a toast. "And here's to the next project," Jen said. "The baby shower."

Everybody groaned, and Jen laughed. "Come on, we're almost done. We can do it. Mrs. Russo and Mrs. Grover have been cooking for days, and we're just about there."

"Whew," Joe said. "I really can't wait until this is all over."

Another round of "here, here's" sounded with a couple of groans, and Jen laughed, looking forward to that herself.

CHAPTER 21

After the chairs had been delivered and the food stowed in the refrigerator for the shower the next day, Carrie stepped into Mrs. Grover's small but cozy home. The warmth of the fireplace filled her with a feeling of contentment and safety. Mrs. Grover sat at the kitchen table, her light blue eyes twinkling as she carefully looked through old photographs from her high school days.

She looked up as Carrie entered, her gaze warm and welcoming. "Come in, my dear," she said, gesturing to the chair across from her. "I was just looking at these old pictures. It brings back such wonderful memories."

Carrie smiled, setting her bright blue sparkly handbag down on the table. She wasn't exactly sure why Mrs. Grover was going through a photo album when Earl would pick her up any minute for the reunion, but she was interested. "Oh, please do share!" she said. "I'd love to see a picture of you."

Mrs. Grover nodded, eagerly picking up one photo and pointing to a girl in the center. "That was me, right there," she said, her voice filled with nostalgia. "We had such a grand time those days. I still miss it sometimes. But that was all before."

Carrie waited for Mrs. Grover to continue, but she didn't. Mitzie came into the room and glanced at the photo album. She sat down beside her sister and rested her hand on the photo album.

"Althea, before was before. Yes, it was awful. Yes, it was a raw deal, but to tell you the truth, I don't remember you being this happy even then. Even before."

Mrs. Grover's bright blue eyes sparkled with tears, and Carrie was positive she'd missed something, but at the same time, was dying to ask. Before what? Her gaze met Mitzie's, and Mitzie smiled softly.

"We've been talking today about happiness and missed opportunities, and the way we thought life was going to turn out."

"Oh," Carrie said. "Things sure do change, that's for sure."

Mitzie nodded. "They do. And things that happened long ago can still fill our hearts, Althea. That was all fifty years ago. You deserve to be happy now."

Mrs. Grover blinked a few times, as if coming out of a daze. "Thank you, Mitzie. I could never just have fun like you did. But I think I'm ready to try now."

Mitzie smiled and patted her sister's hand. She closed the photo album and put it back in its place on the bookshelf. "Go wipe those tears away. Earl will be here in no time, and I'm sure he's aiming to have a good time."

Carrie waited until Mrs. Grover left the room before whispering to Mitzie, "Before what? What happened?"

Mitzie shook her head and whispered, "Right after college, Althea fell in love. Hard. First and last time, I'm afraid, as they got married and he was immediately shipped off overseas. Never came back. She's been alone ever since. Much as I've tried to change that. Hasn't worked. Until now."

"Oh, gosh," Carrie said, overcome with the sadness that Mrs. Grover must have felt all these years. "So why does she seem so sad? If she's happy about Earl?"

Mitzie shrugged. "I don't know. Maybe she's finally saying goodbye to Richard. She never really did back in the day, when she should have."

Carrie smiled when Mrs. Grover returned to the living room, her lipstick freshened up and a smile back on her face.

"Thank you, Mitzie. You're right. It's been long enough."

She turned to Carrie and smiled, reaching for the beaded green handbag. "Oh, Carrie, this is beautiful!"

"I brought it for you. It's bright and cheerful, and I hope you're going to have a wonderful evening."

Mrs. Grover's eyes widened as she reached out to touch the bag. "Oh, my! Thank you, Carrie," she said, reaching out for a hug.

"Looks like it's just my style," Mitzie said with a smile.

"Well, looks like it might be Mrs. Grover's style now, too."

Mrs. Grover pulled back from her hug and placed her hand on Carrie's cheek. "Please, Carrie, call me Althea. All of you girls, please. It's time to retire Mrs. Grover, don't you think?"

Mrs. Grover—Althea—hugged her sister, too. She looked in the mirror one more time and smiled at what she saw.

Carrie wiped away a tear and took a deep breath. Jen cracked the door after a quick knock and said, "Can I come in? I think I'm missing all the fun."

Mrs. Grover gestured for her to come in, and Jen actually almost missed a step when she saw Mrs. Grover. "You look spectacular, Mrs. Grover," she said, giving Mrs. Grover a hug.

Carrie cleared her throat. "Althea," she said, lifting her eyebrows.

"Oh, okay," Jen said. "I'd like to take some pictures. This is a big day, and I want to capture this moment for posterity."

Mrs. Grover blushed as Jen snapped away, capturing her in a lovely blue dress that brought out the color of her eyes.

"You look stunning, Althea," Carrie said.

Mrs. Grover fidgeted with the handbag. "I don't know why I'm so nervous. It's just a high school reunion. I'm sure everyone else will look just as old and wrinkly as I do," she said with a chuckle.

Carrie and Jen exchanged a knowing smile. "I'm sure you'll be the belle of the ball, Althea," Jen said, adjusting her phone camera settings.

As they were getting ready, they heard a car pulling up outside. Carrie peeked through the window and saw a sparkling white convertible. "Oh my goodness, who's that?" she exclaimed.

"It's Earl," Jen said, and they rushed outside to see him in a sharp suit stepping out of a shiny white convertible.

"Oh, my," Mrs. Grover said, her eyes lighting up.

Earl walked over, grinning from ear to ear.

"Earl," Jen began. "Wherever did you get that car? I've only seen your beat-up truck."

"I'm a man of mystery, ladies. There's a lot you don't know about me. But Althea knows," he said, reaching for Mrs. Grover's hand. "You look lovely, my dear. And that dress, it is stunning," he said, his eyes twinkling as he slipped a white corsage over her wrist.

Mrs. Grover blushed as Carrie and Jen took more pictures. "Thank you, Earl. You look quite dashing yourself," she said, admiring his fancy suit.

As Earl helped Althea into the car, Mitzi, Jen, and Carrie stood on the stoop, watching how caring Earl was with Mrs. Grover. When they were out of earshot, Carrie told Jen what had happened before she had arrived. "That's a real tearjerker, isn't it?" Carrie asked.

"Wow. Sure is. You never really know what's going to happen, do you? I'm so happy she met Earl," Jen said.

Carrie nodded. "Yes, and that she was willing to step

out of her comfort zone. I think most of her life, she'd been hiding behind those curtains. Who knows what would have happened if she hadn't been brave?"

"True," Jen said. "Or if you hadn't barged in that day to spy on the open house."

Carrie laughed and nodded.

"Do you think they'll get married?" Mitzi asked, a hopeful look on her face.

Carrie shrugged. "Who knows? They're clearly smitten with each other. Anything could happen."

They watched as the convertible drove off into the distance, Mrs. Grover waving goodbye. "Good luck, Mrs. Grover! Have a wonderful time," Carrie called out.

"I thought we were supposed to call her Althea," Jen said, frowning.

Carrie shrugged. "That'll take some getting used to, I think."

As they walked back inside, Carrie and Jen both let out a sigh. "I hope we're still in love like that when we're their age," Jen said, a wistful look on her face.

Carrie smiled. "I really wasn't expecting to find somebody for a second time around."

Jen nodded. "Neither was I. I guess we're all pretty lucky. And I hope we're still this lucky when we're their age."

"Me, too," Carrie said as they walked back to Jen's house for the next event.

CHAPTER 22

"I'm so tired that I don't remember my name," Carrie said as she rested her head on one of Jen's beach chairs.

"It's Carrie," Dirk said and pulled her up. "I agree, and I need to hit the hay if we're going to set everything up tomorrow morning."

"I'm going to head up to bed," Faith said. "In fact, I think I'll take a bath first. My muscles aren't going to recover, I don't think."

Jen laughed and hugged them both as they went their separate ways. "Thanks for everything, guys. I'll figure out some way to repay you."

Both Faith and Carrie held up a hand and waved as they walked away, looking as tired as Jen felt. She turned to Joe, who looked like he'd fallen asleep in his deck chair.

"Joe?" she whispered, and she squealed when he

grabbed her and sat her on his lap, planting a kiss on her cheek.

"Yes?" he asked.

She settled in, resting her head on his shoulder.

"So, what do you think of Mrs. Grover and Earl?" Jen asked.

Joe responded with a playful smile. "I must say, they are quite the remarkable couple. Perhaps we could learn a thing or two from them. They sure do seem to be enjoying life."

Jen laughed lightly. "Are you implying that we don't?"

Joe gave a nonchalant shrug. "No, not at all. I was referring more to their willingness to just embrace life. Knowing what they want and just forging ahead."

Jen paused, taking a moment to collect her thoughts before responding. "It is a big deal. I can tell they're happy, but things have happened pretty fast."

Joe nodded in agreement, reaching for her hand. "I concur. But ultimately, life is too short to waste time not being with someone who brings you joy."

Jen looked at him, feeling a warmth in her chest. "That's true. It's interesting that something that in some ways seems fast really isn't, in a bigger perspective. Depends on how you look at it. I'm truly grateful that we met up again, Joe."

Joe smiled back at her, pulling her into a hug. "Well, I would never have known it from the last few weeks. You've been a tad more than stressed."

She nudged his arm. "That had nothing to do with you. The shower, the house—you know. It was a lot."

"I could tell," he said, his smile evident even in the darkness. "But I hope you're happy now."

Jen sighed and rested her head on his shoulder again. "I am. Very happy. And I can't imagine it ever being any better."

He squeezed her hand and kissed the top of her head. "I'm happy with you too, Jen. And the same for me. Seems like it's been like this forever. And I never want it to stop." He paused for a moment, then said, "Even though it's been a lot of work and my hands are raw."

"Oh no," she exclaimed, sitting up and smacking him on the arm.

Just then, they heard a car pulling up outside. Mrs. Grover and Earl walked up to the porch, smiling and waving. "Hello, Jen, Joe. We had a wonderful time at the reunion," Mrs. Grover said, a twinkle in her eye.

Jen and Joe exchanged a knowing look. "We could tell that you were going to have a great time," Joe said with a grin.

"See you tomorrow, bright and early," Mrs. Grover said as she took Earl's arm, and they headed back toward her house. Mrs. Grover and Earl chuckled as they went inside, closing the curtains.

Jen smiled. "Well, look at that. No curtain twitching from Mrs. Grover—Althea. Not tonight, anyway."

They sat in silence for a moment, Jen's heart full with

all the changes. "I'm looking forward to the shower tomorrow," Jen said finally, breaking the silence.

Joe nodded, a smile on his face. "Me too. It's been a lot of work, but it'll be worth it to see Amber and Michael happy. We'll all have a great time."

"You're joking, right?" Jen asked, not sure whether or not she should believe him.

"Nah, not joking. The guys plan to hold down the deck for you while you're having the shower. Michael called and asked if we'd keep him company since he's driving Amber out. Didn't think you'd mind."

"Of course not," Jen said. And it warmed her heart that her son wanted to be with Joe—Joe was the one he'd called—while they were honoring his wife, his baby, and the next generation. Everything truly seemed in order.

CHAPTER 23

Althea had expected the evening to be nice, but not as wonderful as it had turned out. They'd shared a wonderful evening of dancing and catching up with Earl's old friends, and he had taken great care to introduce her to everyone—as his date, no less. In the beginning, a few of his friends had seemed unsure about the two of them. After all, Earl's wife had been his high school sweetheart and these people had all known her, so she was grateful that they treated her with such respect and courtesy. They clearly respected Earl, and she wasn't surprised, as he was such a kind man.

He'd kissed her lightly after he'd parked in front of her house, and she was a bit surprised when he asked to come in. Any normal night, she'd have gladly invited him in. But it had been different since Mitzie had arrived.

She glanced at her watch and up at the second story of

her house—Mitzie's bedroom light was off, so it was likely a safe bet.

Once inside, Althea turned on the kettle and started tea while Earl stood silently, his hands in his pockets while he circled the living room. Althea was relieved that there wasn't much noise, and that Mitzie wouldn't be joining them for once. As she set up the tea tray, she watched silently as Earl picked up and inspected the pictures on her mantel one by one.

Her's house was small but comfy, with pictures of her deceased husband on the mantelpiece that she dusted every day. In all the times that Earl had been over to visit, he'd never pressed her about any of them, and she had volunteered no information, either.

She set the tea tray on the table and sat down beside Earl on the sofa. He reached for her hand and rubbed the petals of the corsage he'd brought between her fingers. In all the weeks they'd spent together, he'd never been this quiet. In fact, between Keith and Earl, Althea marveled that she ever got a word in edge wise. She'd gotten to know him very well over that time and knew that when he wanted to talk about something a little more serious, he often took his time getting there, working his way up to it.

And she wasn't wrong about that. Earl took a sip of his tea, kissed her on her cheek and leaned back on the sofa, his warm hands taking hers. And he began to tell her about his deceased wife.

Althea listened intently—she'd been wanting to ask, but

had also wanted to wait until he was ready to talk about it. He described how they'd met, married, and made a life together. How well they got along, that she was a good cook—but added that Althea was a much better one, and she blushed—and that they'd been very happy.

"Althea, I realized at the reunion that everyone there loved my wife. And I did, too. But that was then and this is now, and they loved you, too. And so do I."

His hands tightened over hers, and she was glad of it, because she was afraid they might be shaking. It had been years—no, decades—since she'd given up all hope of finding someone to spend her life with. And the years had passed in front of her as the hope grew more and more faint. Until finally, she hadn't had any left.

Until now. "Oh, Earl," she said, feeling her blush and glad that Mitzie wasn't there to see it. And point it out to everybody. "I'd given up finding anyone at all, let alone someone I could fall in love with, like you."

Earl sat up straight and looked like a little boy who'd been given an extra piece of cake after supper. His smile brightened the room, and her heart threatened to jump out of her chest.

He nodded slowly and held her hands a little more tightly as he turned to her and slid onto one knee, wincing as he did. "Tonight when I saw you, I was dazzled by your beauty. And dancing with you in my arms—well, I could have stayed all night. And I realized something, like a flash of lightning. I realized that I wanted to spend the rest of my life with you," Earl said. "You make me so happy, I love being with you. I'm almost afraid to ask, but will you marry me?"

Althea tried to speak, but words wouldn't come. Tears sprung up, and she rested her palm on this very dear man's cheek, and she'd never felt so much love in her life. Never.

"Althea? Are you all right?" he asked her, his face concerned.

She laughed for a moment and found her voice. "I am definitely all right. I've never been happier. And of course I'll marry you, Earl. I would be proud and honored to be your wife."

Earl let out a sigh of relief and kissed her palm, holding her hand in both of his. "You've made me the happiest man alive. But I have to apologize—I don't have a ring yet."

Althea helped him up and back onto the couch, sitting back down but a little closer this time.

"I don't care about that. I just can't wait to be your wife."

They discussed the type of wedding they wanted, and Althea assured Earl that she didn't care. It didn't matter to her at all. The smaller and sooner, the better.

Earl agreed and looked at her with a sly grin. "How about Vegas? Tomorrow? We can take the convertible."

Her eyes flew open wide, and she smiled at him. "It's perfect. Just perfect. And let's not tell anyone," she said, pointing toward the upstairs bedroom. The last thing she wanted was Mitzie to laugh about it—or worse, try to talk her out of it. Her mind was made up, and she hadn't been this excited about anything in her whole life.

Earl frowned for a moment. "I think that's all right. But I'd feel pretty awful not telling Keith."

"Oh," Althea said, a nudge of worry appearing. "I agree. He needs to know. You don't think he'll be upset, do you?"

Earl laughed and stood. "No. Not at all. In fact, he'll be glad. He knows how I feel about you, and I bet he'll actually be a bit relieved. I haven't talked about anything else besides you for months."

Relief swept over Althea as she wrapped her arms around Earl's neck, planting a sweet kiss on his smiling lips. "I'm so glad. It wouldn't be all right with me if he objected."

"Not a chance. I know my boy. He knows a good thing when he sees it. Just like his dad."

Althea rested her head on Earl's shoulder and smiled. "He's one smart kid, that one."

Earl nodded and headed for the door. "Tomorrow, then?" he asked with his hand on the door.

Althea smiled and nodded before she realized that tomorrow was Amber's baby shower. There was no way she could miss that—they'd been planning for weeks. Earl, too.

They decided to leave right after the shower, early in the afternoon. Earl kissed her goodbye, and as she closed the door behind him, she took a moment to take in what had just happened. She picked up a picture of her Richard and told him that she was very happy. She knew in her heart that he would be happy for her, and she set the picture down gently, knowing she might not spend as much time with it as she had in the past.

CHAPTER 24

The sun was shining brightly, and the birds were chirping as Jen stepped out of her beach house, ready to tackle the big day - the one they'd all been working toward for weeks. She padded down the stairs in her slippers and gasped, almost as if the sight of the finished remodel was brand new. She'd been looking at contractors' tools for so long she'd forgotten how big and roomy it all was. And now - she just couldn't believe the transformation.

She quickly made two pots of coffee, filling any thermos she could find, knowing that coffee would be necessary as soon as everybody arrived to help set up. She checked the refrigerator for anything to add to the coffee—nope, it was still as empty as it had been last night when she went to bed. But it did hum, and it was music to Jen's ears. It'd be full soon enough.

Back upstairs, she got dressed and knocked on Faith's door. "It's morning, Faith. Up and at 'em."

She laughed when she heard Faith groan - just like she had when her grandmother had said the same words to her when she was a teenager. Everyone arrived, some of them yawning and still rubbing sleep out of their eyes, and before Jen knew it, she was making two more pots of coffee. But they got all the tables set up, chairs out, and the buffet and gift tables ready to go. Dirk helped Carrie with the decorations she'd bought, and Jen shook her head. It really was lovely—and not orange and green.

"Nice decorations, Carrie. Really pretty," Faith said, eyeing the two gigantic bouquets of pink flowers that Carrie had brought, one for each table. "These are gorgeous."

"Aw, thanks," she said. "Bethany helped me pick them out, actually. I wanted daffodils and daisies. Orange, of course, but Bethany said I should stick with pink and blue." She adjusted one of the vases and nodded with satisfaction.

"Thank goodness for Bethany," Faith whispered to Jen, and they both laughed. Jen said, "It was a pretty big risk giving her decorations. Yay for Bethany."

"Where do you want these ice chests, Jen?" Joe asked, pointing toward three very big ones that Jen had filled the day before.

"The two blue ones go inside the door, right there." She pointed to the spot where she wanted them. "The big red one is for you guys. Out on the deck."

Joe raised his eyebrows and opened the chest, smiling

and throwing her a thumbs up as he checked out the contents. "Aw, thanks. Perfect," he said as he carried it outside. Mrs. Grover and Mrs. Russo arrived with the food - the lasagne smelled divine, and Jen popped the trays and the garlic bread in her brand new oven and turned it on low. Mrs. Grover put the enormous bowls of salad in the refrigerator, and Jen laughed.

"What?" Mrs. Grover asked, looking a little distracted.

"Oh, nothing. It's just your salad is the very first thing to go into my new refrigerator. It's so exciting," Jen said, her eyes twinkling.

Mrs. Grover smiled and said, "Oh, yes. It's lovely. Earl certainly did a fine job on the remodel."

Jen raised her eyebrows, knowing Earl hadn't done the whole thing himself, but she guessed that's what love sounded like. Mitzie had claimed the corner by the fireplace to set up her games, eager to get started. "These are so much fun. The girls are going to love them," she said, squirting something that looked dark and runny into a diaper. She hoped it was chocolate and didn't even want to ask what game it was for. She had way too much to do and just had to trust Mitzie on that one.

Just as they were getting into the swing of things, the phone rang. Jen took a breath when she saw it was Greta, curious about what she could be calling for, but at the same time grateful that everything was in order, and whatever it was, it wouldn't matter, just as she'd hoped.

Jen answered and could tell that Greta was in tears.

"Jen, I dropped the cake!" she cried. "I was so excited to host the shower, and now it's ruined. I'm devastated."

Jen paused for a moment, surprised that Greta was so upset. When everything had happened at the wedding, Greta didn't seem to even notice, let alone mind. But Jen could tell that she was genuinely upset, and she quickly reassured Amber's mom, telling her that everything was going to be okay. "Don't worry, Greta," she said. "I'll take care of it. Just come to the shower and enjoy yourself. That's what this day is all about."

Jen took a second to wonder how Greta hadn't been able to produce even one small thing for the shower. She did know that Greta had a full-time job - a big one that took a lot of time - and she glanced around the room for a moment. Dirk and Carrie laughed as they argued over how the tablecloths should hang. Faith and Gene counted out the tables and made sure they all had the right number of chairs. Mrs. Russo and Mrs. Grover were tussling over what should go where on the buffet table. Mitzie arranged the games in the order she wanted them to be played, happy in her own world. And she could see Joe through the new windows, re-arranging the deck chairs for his part of the excitement. Keith and Earl were absent, but she knew they would join Joe later, and they'd certainly done enough to get ready even before this day.

She realized that this whole thing had taken almost an army - an army of friends, but still an army. Jen could never have done any of this on her own - including saving the day for Michael and Amber's wedding. She'd had Carrie and Faith for that and was never on her own.

Her heart tugged for Greta - maybe she didn't have friends she could rely on, and compassion washed over her. She went into the garage and rummaged through some boxes to find everything she needed to make several batches of Nana's blueberry muffins as dessert for the shower. They'd be good, and she could make them look pretty on a platter. And that way Nana could join them too. So maybe the big cake with the teddy bear on it wouldn't even be missed.

CHAPTER 25

Jen walked around the party, admiring the decorations and feeling a sense of pride. Amber's baby shower was turning out to be a great success, despite the challenges they'd faced in putting it together. The beach house was decorated with balloons and streamers in shades of pink and blue, with a table set up to display the gifts. The guests chatted and laughed, and the guys who had stayed after helping to set up were out on the porch, sipping beers and toasting to a job well done.

Jen made her way over to the food table, which was filled with delicious treats. There were blueberry muffins, which she had made that morning, along with a variety of sandwiches, chips, and dips along with the lasagna, salad and garlic bread. A large pot of freshly brewed coffee was keeping warm on a hot plate, and a pitcher of ice water sat on the table, ready for anyone who needed a drink.

As she was admiring the food, Amber approached her, a smile on her face.

"Jen, this is amazing," she said, giving her a hug. "I can't believe you pulled this off in such a short amount of time."

Jen smiled, feeling a sense of satisfaction. "I'm just glad it's going well," she said. "I wanted this to be special for you."

Amber looked around the room, taking in the decorations and the guests. "It is special," she said. "I couldn't have asked for anything more."

Just then, Greta approached, looking upset. "Jen, can I talk to you for a moment?" she asked, her voice trembling.

Jen nodded, sensing that something was wrong. She led Greta over to a quiet corner of the room and listened as she apologized again about the cake she had promised to bring.

Jen grabbed her hand and pulled her outside, on the back deck where they could talk in private.

"Greta, don't worry about it," Jen said, placing a comforting hand on her arm. "Everyone makes mistakes. And besides, the muffins I made are a hit. People will barely even notice the missing cake."

Greta sniffed and nodded, her eyes filling with tears. "I just feel so embarrassed," she said.

Jen gave her a hug. "Don't be," she said. "You're here, and that's what matters. And who knows, maybe the cake would have fallen on the way here anyway."

Greta laughed through her tears and gave Jen another hug. "Thank you," she said. "You always know just what to say. And what to do." She shook her head in amazement. "You have everything under control, and I'm just a mess. How do you do that? Keep it all together?"

"If she only knew," Jen thought, thinking of the army of friends it had taken to put this all together. She wouldn't have been able to do it without a single one of them, and she told Greta so. "I could never have done any of this on my own. I have great friends who stepped up, and I'm just glad it worked. For Amber."

"I wish I had that much backup. I always try to be in control of everything, and then in the end, I can't do it. I really admire you, Jen. You can let people help. I hope to be able to do that someday."

Jen's breath hitched as she realized that Greta was right. She really did give up control, letting friends help, and she thought maybe it was a new era for her.

Jen smiled and squeezed Greta's hand reassuringly. "Well, if it makes you feel better, I was pretty much winging this party," she confessed with a laugh. "It wasn't as organized as it might seem."

Greta smiled and wiped her eyes. "I guess we all have our moments," she said in agreement. Then she turned towards the door leading back inside the beach house and took a deep breath before pushing it open with renewed determination.

Inside, Amber waited for them with a bright smile on her face and a glass of sparkling cider in each hand. She handed one to her mother and one to Jen, reaching for one herself with an encouraging nod before clinking glasses with both of them in celebration of all their hard work being done right on time despite the last-minute hiccups along the way.

Jen and Greta went back into the living room, arm in arm. The guests chatted and laughed, the smell of food and coffee filling the air. Jen watched as Amber opened her gifts, a look of joy on her face.

As the party wound down, the guests said their goodbyes and headed home. Jen, Faith, and Carrie cleaned up, feeling a sense of satisfaction at a job well done.

"This was perfect," Amber said, giving Jen a hug. "Mitzie's games were hilarious, and everybody had a great time. I can't thank you enough."

Jen smiled, feeling a sense of pride. "It was my pleasure," she said. "I just wanted to make this a special day for you."

As they said goodnight, Jen couldn't help but feel grateful for the friends and family in her life. Despite the challenges they had faced, the party had been a success, and that was all that mattered. And as she thought about the food, the decorations, and the laughter, she knew that this was a day that they would all always remember.

CHAPTER 26

The white chairs they had rented had been folded and stacked, all the leftovers were in the fridge, and the brand-new tile floor swept. Jen looked around her new kitchen and living room and couldn't believe how things had turned out.

Joe came up behind her and wrapped his hands around her waist, nuzzling her neck.

"Are you happy?" he asked, and she wasn't sure if she had the words to tell him just how happy she was.

She turned and kissed him. "I don't think I've ever been this happy," she said. "And it's all thanks to you."

He laughed and shook his head. "I'd love to take credit for all this myself, believe me. But you know I can't." He gestured to the deck outside where all the people who had made this happen were enjoying the unseasonably warm and beautiful beach afternoon.

"I am grateful to everybody, I really am. But you led the

charge. And I didn't need to be in control. I didn't even want to be."

"Are you saying that you gave up a little of your—um—in-charge-ness? For lack of a better word?"

She smiled and nodded. "I guess I did. It was eye-opening to realize I trusted you to make this work and didn't feel like I had to do it on my own."

He grabbed her hand and pulled her toward the door. "I'll take eye-opening, but I'd like to talk more about this later. At the moment, though, it appears the party is continuing on the deck."

Jen hadn't sat down in the chair Joe brought for her before Mitzie came tearing down the sidewalk from Mrs. Grover's house.

"Girls, come quick!" Mitzie exclaimed as she bounded up the stairs to the deck.

"What?" Jen asked, as everyone on the deck took still.

"Althea and Earl are eloping to Las Vegas to get married!" Mitzie announced.

Jen, Carrie, and Faith all gasped in shock. They had all grown so close, and Jen couldn't imagine them getting married without their friends and family present.

Jen turned to Keith, her eyes wide. "Did you know about this?" she asked.

Keith shook his head and held up his palms. "No, ma'am. Not really. Nothing. Nope. Nada. First I've heard of it. But you know, my old man, when he gets his mind made up, look out. And I can say that I know he thinks Mrs. Grover is the cat's meow."

Jen giggled and looped her arm through Keith's. She'd become quite fond of him and Earl through this entire process — they were practically family.

"And you'd be okay with that?" she asked gently. Joe had laughed at her comment about people getting married and the opinions of their adult children, but she wanted to make sure.

He nodded as quickly as she'd ever seen him. "Absolutely. One hundred and twenty percent. I know my dad's ornery, but it's usually only when he's hungry, and Mrs. Grover makes sure to take care of that. She makes him happy, and that makes me happy. Definitely. Absolutely. And to be honest, I'd like to be there to see them tie the knot. Strap on the old ball and chain. Seal the deal."

Jen smiled and squeezed his arm. "Then we have to do something," Jen said. "We can't let them get married in Las Vegas without us. We have to convince them to get married here."

"Yes!" Carrie agreed. "We have all the chairs, food, and decorations from the baby shower. We can make it a beautiful beach wedding for them."

Dirk added, "It would be easy to set up. We don't return the chairs until tomorrow, and all the decorations are still up."

Faith laughed, pointing at the helium balloons printed with teddy bears. "Maybe we could at least take down the ones that aren't— you know—relevant."

"Most of them are, though," Carrie said. "I made sure to make them just pink and blue since we didn't know if the baby would be a boy or a girl. We can use the pink ones."

"And we can help Mrs. Grover get ready with something old, something new, something borrowed, and something blue," Faith added.

The three friends quickly bounded down the steps and headed next door to Mrs. Grover's house. When they arrived, Althea and Earl were sitting in the living room, holding hands, and looking at wedding magazines.

"Althea, Earl," Jen said as she walked in. "We heard the news and we couldn't be more excited for you two. But we have a proposition for you."

"What is it?" Althea asked, her eyes lighting up with curiosity.

"We want to host your wedding on the beach in front of my house," Jen said. "We have all the chairs, food, and decorations from the baby shower. We can make it a beautiful beach wedding for you and Earl. Tonight. Right now."

"But we want to elope," Earl said, looking a bit confused. "We don't want a big fuss."

"We know, but we want to be there for you," Carrie said. "We want to witness your love for each other and celebrate with you. And we want to help Althea get ready with something old, something new, something borrowed, and something blue."

"And we have so many sentimental reasons for why we want to be there for you," Faith added. "We all care about you two so much, and we want to be a part of this special moment in your lives."

Tears welled up in Mrs. Grover's eyes as she listened to her friends. She had not had many close friends in her life, and the thought of having them there to support her on her wedding day was overwhelming.

"I don't know what to say," Althea said, her voice shaking. "I never thought I'd have friends like you in my life. I don't know what to say."

"We know you don't want a fuss," Jen said, "but it really won't be. We have everything we need to do this tonight, before the sun sets. And we promise you that we'll make it a beautiful and memorable day for you and Earl. And we can all be here to celebrate you. Keith, Mitzie, all of us. We don't want to miss it."

Mrs. Grover looked over at Earl, who was smiling at her. She took a deep breath and made her decision.

"Okay," Mrs. Grover said, her voice filled with happiness. "Let's do it. Let's get married on the beach, Earl. With everybody we love."

CHAPTER 27

The surprise on Joe, Dirk, and Keith's faces when Carrie announced the news was priceless. If they hadn't been the awesome guys they were, Jen was pretty sure they'd have run for the hills.

"We're setting up an impromptu wedding for Earl and Mrs. Grover," Carrie said, beaming. "They're getting married today."

Joe, Dirk, Gene, and Keith all looked at each other in disbelief. "What do you mean, they're getting married today?" Joe asked.

"We mean they're getting married today," Jen said, with a laugh. "And we're going to make it happen."

"But how?" Dirk asked, looking around the beach. "We don't have anything set up. We don't even have an arch."

"That's where we come in," Jen said, with a twinkle in her eye. "We're going to make this happen. We'll find an arch, set up the chairs we already have, and make sure everything is perfect for the happy couple."

"It just makes sense," Carrie added. "We don't want them to get married without us, and we have everything ready right here. And I'm sure nobody would mind having leftovers from lunch. We've got Mrs. Russo's famous lasagna."

Dirk laughed and rubbed the back of his neck. "By the time this weekend's over, I'm going to be strong enough to qualify for the Olympics in something."

"Yeah, maybe thumb hitting," Joe said, nudging Dirk with his elbow. "Okay, come on, guys. Let's get these chairs set up. And try to find something for an arch. And I guess some music."

"Oh, I can do that," Faith said. "I have some outdoor speakers and can make a quick playlist. For the wedding and for after."

Joe glanced at Keith, whose eyes were wide. "You in, Keith?"

Keith nodded vigorously. "Yeah. I'm in. All in. You know, my dad can be ornery, and Mrs. Grover makes him less ornery, so I'm all for it."

"Okay, then. Keith, let's go make an arch. We can swing by the hardware store real fast," Gene said, and Keith stood up, ready to go. "Faith, do you have any type of gauzy, white something we could - I don't know - dress it up with?"

"I sure do," Faith said. "I'll grab some out of the shop.

Carrie, can you and Dirk decorate it? Those pink bouquets would look perfect on each side."

"Wait a minute," Joe said before everyone headed off for their assigned tasks. "Aren't we forgetting something? The most important thing? Who's going to officiate this ceremony?"

Carrie stood and cleared her throat, her thumbs holding the lapels of her sweater. "May I introduce you to the Most Reverend Minister Carrie Westland? Or something like that. I have one of those internet certificates."

Jen looked at Carrie, incredulous. "You? When did you get that?"

Carrie shrugged. "I don't know. I was bored one night and thought it would be fun. Never imagined I'd actually use it. And for something so fun."

Jen shook her head. "Wow. Amazing." She glanced at Joe, and he shrugged.

"How many chairs should we put out?" Joe asked, two chairs in each hand.

"Let's go down and pick a spot on the beach and decide where the arch will be. And where I'll stand. It's all so exciting," Carrie said, grabbing a couple of chairs.

Dirk and Jen did the same, following Joe and Carrie down toward the shoreline. Keith and Gene showed up not much afterward with a lovely arch, and Keith said he needed to go home and change.

"I guess I'm standing up for Pop today. He said he wanted me to be his best man. I need to go get cleaned up.

At least give it a try," Keith said as he turned toward his truck. "See you guys in an hour."

Faith and Gene looked at the arch and set the bouquets on each side. Gene held a stepladder for Faith, and Jen smiled as they laughed together, trying to get the wind to cooperate with them and the white gauze.

Jen grabbed Carrie's hand and said, "Let's go see how it's going with Althea. She might need some help, and I want to see her. I just have to grab something from the house real quick. Wait here."

Jen ran up the stairs to her bedroom and opened her jewelry box, looking for the perfect thing. When she found it, she put it in her pocket and ran back downstairs to grab some scissors. She scouted Nana's rose garden, clipping the most perfect blooms and headed back to Mrs. Grover's.

Carrie nodded, and they headed to Mrs. Grover's. "Come in!" Mrs. Grover's voice called out.

Jen opened the door, and she and Carrie slipped into the living room, where Mrs. Grover was sitting in a chair while her sister Mitzie piled her white hair into pretty swirls, pinning them tightly.

"Althea," Jen exclaimed. "You look so pretty!"

Mrs. Grover smiled, but Mitzie smiled bigger. "Thank you. I can't believe this is happening," she said.

"We can't either," Carrie said, sitting next to Mrs. Grover.

"I brought you something," Jen said, and she handed Mrs. Grover the bouquet of roses.

Mrs. Grover took the roses and breathed in their sweet

scent. "These are beautiful," she said. "Your Nana's garden always had the loveliest roses."

Jen nodded. "I'm glad you like them. I can wrap them up for a perfect bouquet."

"Thank you. I hadn't even thought of those kinds of details," Mrs. Grover said.

Mitzie finished Althea's hair and stepped back to admire her handiwork. "You look stunning, sis," she said.

Mrs. Grover beamed. "Thank you, Mitzie."

Jen held out a small box. "And I also brought you something old, something new, something borrowed, and something blue. All in one."

Mrs. Grover took the box and opened it. Inside was a sapphire bracelet that had belonged to her dear friend, Jen's grandmother.

Mrs. Grover's eyes filled with tears as Jen clasped it on her wrist. "Oh, Jen," she said. "Thank you so much. I wish she could be here to see this. She'd be in shock."

Jen hugged Mrs. Grover. "I wish she could too, Althea. And I think we're all in shock."

Carrie wiped away a tear. "I'm just so emotional right now. This is such a beautiful moment."

Jen stifled a grin as she'd never seen Carrie quite like this before. Mrs. Grover stood up and hugged her. "Thank you for being here with me, Carrie. It means the world to me. It wouldn't even be happening if you hadn't pushed your way into my house. I wouldn't ever have left."

Jen and Mitzie joined in the hug, and they all stood there for a moment, arms wrapped around each other.

Finally, Jen pulled away. "Well, we should let you get ready. We don't want to be late for the ceremony."

Mrs. Grover nodded. "Thank you again, Jen. And thank you all for being here, making this happen. It's a dream come true, one I didn't even know I had."

As Jen walked back to her house, she couldn't help but feel a warm sense of happiness in her heart. She was so glad that Mrs. Grover had finally come out of her shell and found love again, and she knew that her Nana would have been so happy to see her roses being used for such a special occasion.

CHAPTER 28

Soft, romantic music played as everyone gathered on the beach. Jen was happy to see that Carrie had arrived in a subtle dress that didn't clash with everything else on the beach.

Jen and Joe stood at the back of the chairs, waiting for the others to arrive, and Jen had made sure that Keith, Mitzie, and Althea all knew what they were supposed to do.

Earl drove up in his white convertible and parked right along the boardwalk. He hopped out like he'd never hurt his knee, and there was a spring in his step as he walked up to where they were waiting for him.

He shook Joe's hand. "I just can't thank you all enough. I thought I was going to have Elvis standing up for me, but it turns out it'll be my boy. Doesn't get much better than that."

Joe laughed. "It was a team effort."

Earl nodded as he walked up to the arch and spoke in hushed tones with Carrie. Gene and Dirk were already seated in the front row, and Jen smiled as Mrs. Russo started down the boardwalk with at least a dozen ladies following behind her.

"What's all that?" Joe asked, his eyebrows raised.

Jen turned and squeezed his hand. "I thought Althea might be pleased to have her bridge club here for the special event. They've been playing together for decades. Your mom was all over it and made the calls."

Joe laughed. "I had no idea you were such a romantic," he said, draping his arm over Jen's shoulder. "I might have to up my game."

Jen kissed him on the cheek. "Your game's just fine. I just want it to be a really special day for Althea. She deserves it."

Jen and Joe greeted the ladies, and they took their seats, the warm, soft breeze picking up a bit as the sun began to set. Perfect timing, and a perfect day for a wedding.

"Uh-oh," Joe said as he and Jen looked for their seats in the front row. "What do you think that's about?"

Jen turned and looked in the direction Joe was pointing and rolled her eyes. Faith looked lovely in a soft, flowy skirt, but unfortunately, she was holding Gary's hand as they walked toward the beach.

"Well, I guess she knows what she's doing," Jen said, hoping that Faith actually did.

"Hope so," Joe said as they took their seats.

Althea glowed as she walked down the aisle in her

beautiful white dress, with something old, something new, something borrowed, and something blue—all on one wrist. Earl waited under the arch for his bride, smiling ear to ear. Carrie stepped forward, a broad smile on her face.

"Ladies and gentlemen, we are gathered here today to witness the union of Althea and Earl," she said, her voice ringing out over the beach. "They have come together to make a commitment to each other, to love, honor, and cherish each other for the rest of their lives."

As Carrie spoke, the love between Althea and Earl was palpable. They stood hand in hand, looking into each other's eyes as they exchanged their vows.

"Althea, do you take Earl to be your lawfully wedded husband?" Carrie asked. "Well, maybe lawfully. I'm not exactly sure."

Jen rolled her eyes, and the response in the audience was a mixture of laughter and gasps. But Althea and Earl laughed and carried right on.

"I do," Althea said, her voice filled with love. "Earl, do you take Althea to be your lawfully wedded wife?" Carrie asked.

"I do," Earl said, a smile spreading across his face. As they exchanged their hastily-acquired rings, the audience of friends and family looked on, tears in their eyes.

The ceremony was simple but filled with love and laughter. Faith's playlist provided the perfect background music, and the sound of the waves crashing in the background added to the intimate atmosphere.

When the ceremony was over, Mrs. Grover—not Mrs.

Grover anymore—was all smiles as she introduced her bridge friends to her new husband. The ladies all chattered and congratulated the newlyweds, and Jen heard a steady chorus of, "You didn't even tell us," and "We're thrilled for you."

Jen invited everyone back to the house for a buffet and drinks on the deck. The sun was about to set over the ocean, casting a warm glow over the beach, and it was a perfect chance to celebrate Althea and Earl.

Guests milled around after the ceremony, and Jen and Joe decided to make their way back to the house to set up a little bit for their expected guests. Jen quickly told Carrie what they'd planned, and Carrie said in about ten minutes she'd direct everybody over to the house.

"Oh, good grief," Carrie said, her eyes trained on the backs of Gary and Faith as they walked away.

"Oh no, she can't leave. This is a huge event," Jen said, disappointed that Faith wasn't going to join them.

"I guess we were wrong about that one," Carrie said, gesturing in the direction of Gene, who was also watching Faith and Gary walk away with an equal look of disappointment on his face.

"Well, nothing we can do about it," Carrie said. "I still hope she knows what she's doing. We'll see you back at the house in a few."

Jen nodded, taking Joe's hand and heading back to the house, ready to celebrate Althea and Earl's special day.

CHAPTER 29

Carrie squeezed Jen's hand as Dirk and Joe lit the heaters on Jen's deck. The sun had gone down, and although it had been a perfect warm day for a wedding on the beach, the chill of February was back in the air.

"This worked out great," Carrie said. "I didn't mess up at all, and it was a ready-made reception."

Jen laughed and thought it really hadn't been a mess-up during the ceremony. It was just Carrie, and she loved her for it.

Dirk sat down beside Carrie, draping a sweater over her shoulders. "It really was perfect. The only thing missing was cake."

"Oh," Jen said suddenly as she hopped up. "Carrie, come with me."

Jen went into the garage and picked up the cake she'd gotten for the baby shower and carried it into the kitchen.

"What the heck?" Carrie said as she lifted the top of the

box and peered in. "You got this for the baby shower? Why didn't you bring it out?"

Jen shrugged as she set it on the counter, reaching for forks, plates, and napkins. "Greta really had intended to bring the cake, she just dropped it."

"Like she drops everything," Carrie said, slipping the cake out of the box.

"No, literally. She dropped it."

Carrie laughed and her eyes widened. "Good grief."

"Yeah. And she was so upset and had wanted so badly to do something good for the shower that I didn't have the heart to tell her that I was banking on her—well, dropping it somehow."

"Ah," Carrie said. "Compassionate Jen to the rescue."

Jen shrugged. "I didn't want her to feel worse than she already did. So I just didn't bring it out. I had no idea that we'd be having a wedding and would need a cake."

Carrie looked down at the cake and laughed. "Perfect. I'm sure they'll love a cake with teddy bears that says 'Congratulations Michael and Amber.'"

Jen waved her off. "Get a knife and smooth it over."

"Nah. It's that kind of wedding. They won't care."

Jen nodded, and they took the cake out and set it in front of Earl and Althea, who did indeed not care at all that it had teddy bears on it and someone else's names.

"This is perfect, girls," Althea said as she squeezed Earl's hand. "I couldn't have done any better myself."

Mitzie and Keith both made toasts, to much laughter while the cake disappeared slowly but steadily.

By the time the ladies left after the wedding, Jen was ready to collapse into a deck chair, not that sorry to see them go.

It had been perfect that they'd come, and Althea and Earl were cute, holding court at the head of the table on Jen's deck.

Suddenly, Earl and Althea stood up, their faces lit up with excitement. "We have an announcement to make," Earl said, smiling.

The group of friends turned to face them, eager to hear what they had to say.

"We've decided to go to Las Vegas for our honeymoon," Althea said, a big smile on her face.

"That's amazing," Jen said, giving the couple a hug. "You're going to have the time of your lives."

"We're so happy for you guys," Carrie said. "Las Vegas is the perfect place for a honeymoon."

"Make sure you take lots of pictures," Joe added.

They all laughed when Keith stood and held up his phone. "I'll take care of that. Mitzie and I are going with them."

Althea and Earl thanked everyone for their hard work in making the day perfect for them. As Earl, Mitzie and Keith headed toward Althea's house, she stayed back for a moment.

She took in a deep breath and looked around at her friends on Jen's deck and glanced over at her house, to the window that she'd been peeking out of all those months ago before her life changed forever.

"I don't know how I can ever thank you all for doing this for me. For including me from that first day of the open house and welcoming me into your world. I had no idea mine was so lonely until I met you all. And then it wasn't."

Jen and Carrie hugged Althea and waved as she left, heading toward Las Vegas and her new life.

"That was really something," Joe said as she closed the door behind her, and the sound of Frank Sinatra wafted through her open window.

"It sure was," Jen said.

"Well, I'm going to head out," Gene said, getting up and stretching. "Thanks for letting me help out. It was quite a day. In fact, quite a few weeks," he said, shaking Dirk and Joe's hands and nodding to Carrie and Jen.

Jen stood and gave him a hug. "Thank you, Gene. For being Santa, for pitching in, for—well, everything."

He nodded and smiled before he headed down the boardwalk, finally turning the corner.

It wasn't a few moments before Faith came through the gate of the picket fence, carrying a box of Fig Newtons, of all things.

"Hey," she said, "sorry I missed the reception," as she sat down. "I'm sure it was great."

Jen nodded, wanting desperately to ask what she'd been doing, but she didn't want to put Faith on the spot.

"Where were you?" Carrie asked, her head cocked to one side. "You were supposed to be here."

Faith nodded slowly. "I know. But I had something I had to do."

"More important than this?" Carrie asked, still looking a little annoyed.

"Yeah. Anybody want a Fig Newton?" she asked, holding the box up toward her friends. "You don't have to have one if you don't want to. As it should be."

"No, thank you," Carrie said, sounding a little irritated. "What happened?"

Faith sighed and popped a Fig Newton in her mouth. "Had to kick Gary to the curb. And it's hard to explain, but it took a while. He's not one to take no for an answer."

"Oh," Jen said, her eyebrows raised. She and Carrie exchanged glances and smiles. "Good, Faith. That's good."

Faith nodded and looked at her friends on the deck. "And thanks for not beating me over the head about it. I guess I had to get the picture on my own. Thanks for letting me do that."

Jen nodded, thrilled that Faith had come around. And that they'd trusted her to find that out by herself.

"Well, good you're here now," Carrie said, as she began to tell Faith all about the reception.

Faith laughed and said, "It sounds like it was great."

"It was," Carrie said. "It was the perfect day."

"And Las Vegas is going to be so much fun," Faith added. "I can't wait to see the pictures they bring back."

The group of friends all sat in their deck chairs, relaxing after everything they'd been through in the last few weeks. Jen couldn't imagine how anything could have been more perfect.

And as she gazed out at the ocean, watching the stars twinkle above, she knew that this was just the beginning of a lifetime of love and happiness for Althea and Earl.

EPILOGUE

Faith didn't last much longer and headed up to bed shortly after she had gotten home.

Carrie stood and reached for Dirk's hand, but he didn't move, and his eyes were closed.

"Is he sleeping?" Carrie whispered to Jen.

"If he is, he sure earned it," Joe said with a laugh, nudging Dirk's foot with his own.

"What? Huh, do I have to leave?"

"Yes. It's late." Carrie laughed and pulled harder this time, and he stood and shook his head and rubbed his eyes.

"I don't think I've ever been this tired in my entire life."

"Or sore," Joe added.

"That, too," Dirk said as he followed Carrie down the stairs and out the gate.

Carrie waved to Jen and Joe and held onto Dirk's arm as they headed toward the boardwalk and turned the corner to her house. The wind had died down, and the evening was still, with stars sparkling overhead.

"Man, I was having quite a dream," he said, rubbing his eyes again

"Maybe it was all that cake." Carrie laughed. "What were you dreaming about?"

He shook his head. "I don't remember all of it, but we were at your house, and you wanted me to leave. Felt more like a nightmare."

"You like it at my house?" she asked softly.

He draped his arm around her shoulder. "I do. If it was up to me, I'd never leave."

She stopped and looked at the stars, breathing in the salty air.

He stopped too and turned to look at her. "What?"

"You don't have to if you don't want to. Leave, I mean."

His eyebrows rose, and he stepped closer. "Never?"

She looked down for a moment, feeling a little shy. But she knew what she wanted to say, so she said it.

"No. Never."

He leaned in to kiss her, and his lips tasted sweet. It must have been the cake.

"Does that mean we should talk about graduating from going steady? Maybe get married? It was nice to see Earl and Althea so happy."

Carrie pulled him further on the boardwalk. They were almost at her house, and she stopped again when they reached her front door.

"Yes, they were happy. But we are, too. And you're here

more than at your house. We're practically married, anyway. Why don't you just…"

"Stay?" he asked, his voice soft.

She breathed deeply again, wanting to say something funny, but this didn't seem funny. It seemed right.

"Yes. Please. Forever."

He kissed her again and opened the front door, followed her in, and looked around.

"Okay. Done. Guess I have a house I have to sell."

Carrie laughed as they dropped onto her couch, both of them exhausted.

"Good thing we know a good real estate agent." She smiled as she rested on Dirk's shoulder, thinking there was no place else she'd rather be than with him. Together. Forever.

JEN AND JOE both waved as Dirk and Carrie rounded the corner and headed down the boardwalk.

"I can't believe we pulled this all off," Joe said, shaking his head. "It's a miracle."

Jen laughed and nodded. "It makes me dizzy when I think of all the changes that happened just to get to the shower. And then who would ever have guessed that we'd have a wedding, too?"

"Not me," Joe said. "I was tired after the baby shower, let alone the wedding."

Jen shoved her elbow into his ribs, laughing. "Come on.

It was a beautiful wedding. So exciting for them to start a new life. And so spontaneous. I just can't even imagine."

"I bet. There's no way on this Earth you could ever have done something like that."

"What do you mean? I can be spontaneous if I want to."

He looked at her like she'd just said the silliest thing ever and laughed.

"You're joking, right? You are the least spontaneous person I've ever met. Nothing goes unplanned, it appears."

"That's not fair. We talked about why I feel like I need to make sure things are handled, but that's different than not being…spontaneous."

Joe looked at her and narrowed his eyes. "Really? Okay. I was going to ask you something earlier, but I knew the answer, so I didn't."

"Oh yeah? What?"

"At the wedding—everybody together, spur of the moment, could you have gotten married like that?"

Jen paused for a moment and took in a deep breath. "You mean just in general? Or to you?"

Joe frowned and thought a minute, then turned toward her. "Well, when I asked, I was thinking of in general. But now that you mention it, yeah. To me. Could you have married me on the spur of the moment? You know how much I love you."

"I—oh, gosh. I was not prepared for this conversation," she said slowly. "I—well, it's occurred to me that maybe we're moving a little fast. Don't you think?"

"No, I don't think," Joe said, sounding frustrated. "What

I actually think is that this has been the longest, most drawn-out relationship I've ever known of, for me or anybody else."

Jen didn't seem to understand what he meant. "We've only been back in touch since the beginning of summer. That's less than a year."

Joe hung his head for a moment before speaking. His heart ached with what he wanted to tell her, but he knew it still wasn't a good idea—it hadn't been a good idea when they were in high school, and it wasn't a good idea now. He reached for her hands and held them in his, and the warmth radiated straight into his heart.

"Okay, okay. But if I'd asked you this afternoon to marry me, right then and there, double wedding, could you have said yes?"

Jen thought for a moment, and he worried that the answer would be a flat-out no. It wasn't even an actual proposal. It had started as a simple enough conversation about her being controlling and—how did it get here? But the weight of it had him holding his breath.

She took a deep breath and looked up at the stars, thinking for a moment. "Joe, I love you, too. More than I've ever loved anyone. And I'd love to spend my life with you, if that's what you're asking. I want to grow old with you, like Althea and Earl. And have that much fun."

He breathed a sigh of relief.

"But—" she said.

"Oh, no, a but," he said, hoping she didn't rip the rug from underneath him when his heart was soaring.

She laughed. "Not that kind of but. I was only going to say that the reason I would have was because my kids weren't there. Or my dad. Or even my stinky brother. When I commit my life to you, I want it to be in front of everybody I love, all you guys and my family, too. Like it was for Althea and Earl."

"Whew," he said. "That sounds better than a but."

Jen laughed, pulled him close and kissed him. "Okay, good. But I do have one question for you in return," she said.

"Anything," he said, kissing her again.

She looked up at him, her eyelashes sparkling. "Can I take a rain check?"

He laughed and hugged her, his heart light. "Of course. You just let me know when and I'll be there."

Thank you so much for reading *Newport Nuptials, and I hope you enjoyed it.*

I wrote a special prequel for this series about Jen, Allen, Carrie and Joe when they were all teenagers, soaking up all that's fun in Newport Beach. You can find it here:

https://dl.bookfunnel.com/ta4ai8ek4p

**If you're having any trouble tapping on the prequel, please type

cindynicholsbooks.com/newport-bonus

in your phone or computer browser.

If you'd like to know about new releases, join my mailing list and you'll be the first to know!

Sign up here: Cindy Nichols Newsletter

Turn the page to see more series I've written!

ALSO BY CINDY NICHOLS

Newport Beach Series

Now that her kids are grown, widow Jen Watson and her two life-long best friends are looking forward to a summer of fun at her family's beach house. When Jen's family wants to sell it to developers, Jen and her friends do whatever they can to stop it. A heart-warming series about the bonds of friends and family.

Newport Harbor House (Book 1)

Newport Beginnings (Book 2)

Newport Sunrise (Book 3)

Newport New Moon (Book 4)

A Newport Christmas (Book 5)

Newport Nuptials (Book 6)

The Pearl Beach Series

Julia Montgomery and her husband have run their Shell Shop in the Florida Keys for decades. Well, actually, her husband ran it while she raised the kids. Unexpectedly, she has to figure out how to run it herself, or face the consequences.

The Shell Shop

Shell Shop Secrets

Shell Shop Showdown

Vaquita Beach Series

The Vaquita porpoises in the Sea of Cortez are threatened with extinction, and marine biologist Cassie Lewis has devoted her life to trying to stop that from happening. Join her in this beautiful beach community while she does her best to save the species.

As Deep As the Ocean

As Bright As the Stars

By The Light of the Moon

As Blue As The Sky

River's End Ranch

Several years ago, four very good writer friends and I wrote a really fun sweet romance series, River's End Ranch, all set on a destination guest ranch in Idaho. We rotated publishing, one of us every two weeks, resulting in 60 books in total! It was an amazingly fun experience to write in the same world as some very dear friends: Pamela Kelley, Kirsten Osbourne, Caroline Lee and Amelia Adams. Below are links to the books that I wrote in the series, and two boxed sets of my books in the series.

These are in Kindle Unlimited.

Honest Horseman

Gallant Golfer

Discovering Dani

Mischievous Maid

Christmas Catch-Up 5

Cindy Nichols Box Set 1-4

Snickerdoodle Secrets

Bashful Banker

Mistletoe Mistake

Picture Perfect

Cindy Nichols Box Set 5-8

Teaching Tamlyn

Fanning Flames

Christmas Catch-Up 10

Made in the USA
Middletown, DE
20 March 2023